The
Numinous Protocol

The Alphabet Games

The
Numinous Protocol

Birgit Von Schondorf

authorHOUSE®

AuthorHouse™
1663 Liberty Drive
Bloomington, IN 47403
www.authorhouse.com
Phone: 1-800-839-8640

Published by AuthorHouse   06/14/2012

ISBN: 978-1-4685-8598-8 (sc)
ISBN: 978-1-4685-8599-5 (hc)
ISBN: 978-1-4685-8600-8 (e)

This is a true story, gleaned from a compilation of interviews and dialogue that took place over several years. Names of persons and details of situations have been altered in the name of safety and national security.

Chapter One

Muffled sounds of a third-world country coursed through the wretchedly polluted, bluish air that hung over Islamabad. Mingled with the stench of garbage and excrement, the combination made this city of 1.2 million souls an open-air sewer for anyone unlucky enough to live or have business here.

On this particular day in mid-December, Penn Adams, a CIA operative working undercover, was among the seething mass of people. In an instant, all hell broke loose, and the hunter became the hunted. It was all so surreal, as if the events were happening in slow motion. A violent ballet of chaos—shoving, running, the cacophony of rattletrap automobile horns, shouting. Penn knew he was in imminent danger, and he broke into a sprint, his heart was pounding so hard it felt like it was going to burst through his chest.

"This can't be happening!" his brain screamed out.

His survival instinct kicked in, and he could feel the rush of adrenalin in his veins. He tried to control his breathing, but fear blocked all such efforts. The

ringing in his ears made it hard for him to hear;
close-range gunfire has a tendency to do that.

Penn wondered if he was injured. He couldn't feel
his feet or his bum right knee as he raced down
a shitty little side street. Fifty paces behind him,
several raghead assassins yelling in Urdu, the official
language, pursued and shot at him. He had just
jumped out of a third-floor window. Conveniently,
a pile of sand being used by a construction crew
cushioned his fall.

What an immensely fucked-up day, he thought.

He was certain it would be his last. By the time he
had arrived in Islamabad, he already had used up
more lives than any man was entitled to have. He
was working on . . . five, or was it six? He had lost
count. Segments of his life flashed through his mind
as bullets whizzed past his head. The sound reminded
him of a persistent mosquito hovering near the side
of his head. He could hear the little bastard; he just
couldn't see it.

Up ahead, Penn spotted an old man tending an
ice-cream cart adorned with a skirt that reached down
to the unpaved street, boxes stacked to one side.
Penn ran toward the cart and dove underneath in one
motion, praying that the bearded vendor would not

rat him out to the gunmen who wanted to kill him. Mercifully, they ran past the rickety cart that obscured Penn from their view. His breathing finally began to slow as he knelt motionless.

But Penn was pissed. The extraction team he had been expecting was nowhere to be seen. When he thought the coast was clear, and while still crouched under the cart, he placed a call to Langley on his small satellite phone. He swore at his handler, Clay, to get him the fuck out of Dodge. Sweat ran down his face and into his eyes. He wiped it away with the handkerchief he kept in a back pocket. Then he instructed Clay to relay a call to Aria. He felt like he needed to hear her voice.

In fact, Penn wasn't supposed to be calling anyone in the midst of a mission. But he wasn't sure he would ever get to talk to Aria or see her again. He had just dodged a proverbial bullet; in fact, by sheer luck, he had dodged a hail of them. As far as he was concerned, he had earned the right to break a rule or two.

Clay understood and put the call through without hesitating.

Thursday, November 5th

It should've been a normal day, a day like any other.
Get up, rush like hell, wake up in the shower, struggle
for coffee, swear when you discover on the way to the
car or the train that your stocking has a run in it and
you know that you don't have a backup in your bag.

This day should've been like a mediocre, whiny song
on the radio that now passes for rock with the average
fifteen-year-old in any suburban center in America.

But it wasn't. This was his life, her life, their life, the
country's life, and the agency's life, and there was
nothing normal, standard, or typical about it.

There is no graph or book or sign or special handshake
that ensues when people like them find each other,
sleep together, and fall in love. There's even less to go
on when people like them discover they're far more
connected than meets the eye. So says the day when
they met.

Let's backtrack a bit and talk about when they hadn't
yet met. That could be described easily. Madonna.
Whore. She was Madonna, and he was a whore. She
was now single after being a child bride in an abusive
relationship. She had not been with anyone for a
long time. She was not hot to enter into the bonds of

matrimony—ever again! He, on the other hand, was married and had stayed as such out of guilt, because of their two lovely daughters. He was married to their mother, whom he did not like, much less love or sleep with. He was a whore, getting some on the side like everyone else in his profession—up to double digits a week from a revolving door of four steady women and fillers whenever and wherever. Sport-fucking was his only MO. He was what she now affectionately calls a "himbo." A male bimbo.

Then came that faithful day. That summer day in New York that felt like a blast a of winter. To this day, it still doesn't seem real, but surely it is. It's real. At times too real. Real all over the world. From the Kremlin to Karachi, from Washington and marble halls to sunny beaches. From big rooms with too much technology to men who only have one name and have a closet full of trench coats.

The stakes are so much higher on a normal day than regular people could ever imagine. Doesn't everyone's boyfriend, best friend, soul mate, possible future husband bolt out of bed to take a call in the middle of the night from Karachi? No. No they don't. This is reality, his reality and hers. Aria McConnell remembered what it was like before she met the group, before they knew her and she knew them. Before the meeting that day in New York. She knew everything . . . and Langley knew that, but everyone was doing a damn good job of being in denial. She used to pretend that she was just "some girl." She had gotten the calls years before from family and friends . . . "So sorry—can't make dinner" or "I'm gonna be late" . . . and then an embassy blows up. Total denial.

But back to the day one of the governor's boys, a lawyer, a good for nothing, had the hots for her and facilitated this meeting with him. It was destiny; it had to happen. They would work together. She had already been recruited and had taken on the project. She had given her word. She was the one traveling from the farthest away, but she arrived early. Up at the crack of dawn, a flight to LaGuardia, and a cab into the city.

Security was a pain in her ass. She wished at other times they would be so vigilant. They put some little chicklet through everything short of a full-body cavity search. She felt like she was flying El Al. Or going to Canada, again. Treated like an Escobarian drug lord, you would have thought she was just another hussy blowing someone's boss, but she wasn't.

She was there because of a nun. If anyone would have bothered to ask, she would have been happy to tell them that she was there because of a nun.

When she finally got upstairs to Penn Adam's office, he wanted to jump her, and she knew it. Months later, he confessed that when she walked around the desk, he had the hardest time not manhandling her, deep kissing her, and pushing her down onto the desk. She had him. He was both cocky and scared.

Little did he know, Aria knew who she was dealing with. The only thing she didn't understand was the hug after the business lunch. That was him trying anything to get near her—short of clearing the table there in the steak restaurant and doing her in front of the lunch crowd. They were hot, out of the shoot from the very first moment, and despite the fact that he was so very tuned in because his life depended on it, every minute of every day, he was sunk.

But he was safe because he was with his ultimate match. Like a sidearm that they built for him at Langley. They fit better than a glove. They were twin cells from different times and of a different sex. Like mirror image, twins inside and out on a metaphysical level. It was like two beings existing in one skin. Even standing up was the best sex, times ten. It was all theirs, and no one else ever had a clue.

It was mind-blowing no matter how you looked at it. She was good with all of it by then. She would have been his biggest fan if he would have pulled a Clark

Gable. She could do Scarlet! Probably more Johansen than O'Hara. He told her a month ago that he would have run off to hotel with her that very moment that lunch was over if she would have given him a sign. Ah, then she would have been like the other tarts he was banging from all over the world that were hoping their husband-shopping would come complete with US citizenship.

The animal had stolen the hotshot lawyer's potential girlfriend that he had been bragging about for months. He had not gotten the memo, that this would take time, several months and two trips to the Middle East, one to the Med, and one to the Ottoman Empire, and lastly one moment in Washington. The kicker was getting his chops busted for a relationship with a little blue pill that jumped out of his pocket and onto the carpet. Jumping the gun a bit, no?

They would be very busy for the next few months while he learned about himself, walking into rooms that he'd never known were in the mansion in the first place. In the dark, with no flashlight, he roamed, by braille. Hands first, he bumped his head and toes every day. She watched and tried to be gentle and not giggle. It was hard; he was so very cute all the time. Bet he never thought of himself as cute. But she thought so.

He left her alone on that first trip, alone in
Washington. He was busy freaking out. Completely
freaking out. *Run away . . . Run away.* He was used
to not caring about anyone. They didn't even have sex,
but they wanted to. Aria was glad that they had not
yet slept together. Surely he would have broken her
heart, and of course he did. All she remembered was
being on the treadmill afterwards, feeling terribly hurt,
tears streaming down her face while he drove back
to NYC. She knew he was scared but couldn't believe
that he actually left her there, alone. She wasn't sure
right then that he could make the jump. That he had
the emotional and mental capacity to be able to handle
her. At least he still had no idea what "handling her"
was really about, thank God. He was the one with
handlers, but she was the one who needed them.
Given the time and the headspace, she was hoping
he'd figure this out. That she wouldn't need to hold his
hand too much. She didn't want to be the strong one,
the boy. That always made her feel so unfeminine. She
hated it when she had to take the lead. People were
generally so wishy-washy now, and so ill informed. She
hoped that he would be so wildly intelligent that after
he saw things for himself, and experienced it time and
time again, that he would understand. Telling her that
it was okay. Putting it all together on his own.

She already knew his story. There were just some details to be filled in. But he might think he was completely out of his mind if he really started to understand hers. She hoped not, because she knew this day that she loved him.

Chapter Two

September 14, Tennessee

Underground bunkers, engines, skeezy, low-end VC guys and weapons, big money, and men that only have numbers as names. What am I supposed to feel? My life is like the movies, only much more real. When I don't brush my teeth, I need a lot of mouthwash. That does not happen in the movies, or in the books that I read. The spies in the movies never have bad breath or worry about it. Things always go well. Sean Connery, Roger Moore, Pierce Brosnan, and Daniel Craig are always perfect. Every minute of every day, no basis in reality. The real deal is prep . . . fingers crossed, swear, pray. Closely followed by breathing, amazement, and sleep. This is the real world, not Pinewood. Her Majesty sold separately.

His name was Penn, and he was perfect. At least he was my version of perfect, and that was all that mattered. In a perfect world, I could spell, and my ass would not be broken. That's not so Hollywood. Belly problems based on field stress. Yeah, that's one thing they don't ever show. The big dilemma of the week is how the hell do I introduce all these people to each other without blowing protocol so they can all help each other? Everyone is so sensitive, understandably. I feel like the colorblind kid with the Rubik's cube in my stocking. Duh.

August 16*th*

Sitting here, and it's late. Watching one of my favorite movies, starring one of my favorite actresses—Angela Bassett in *How Stella Got Her Groove Back*. Boy did I need this tonight. We are all alive and intact after these past two weeks . . . amazing!

I am safe, but I have a headache. It's mostly from stress, from having one hell of a night and day and traveling a lot, but I also did something that I don't ever do: I drank. I'm a lightweight to the extreme. An eighth of a glass of red to calm me down and take away the pain in my head and neck. It worked, making me dizzy and providing some necessary relief.

Safety has become an issue again, this time at a really serious level. I get truly dizzy worrying about it. People I love and need at the highest levels, and my abilities at tapping into the brains and energy of the world as I do is very draining and causes me to be dizzy. The noise level inside my head is currently deafening

on a worldwide scale. For months, I have been
amping up without trying to be able to really tune in.
Apparently to be applied, right now. I have something
to contribute, and even if I did not want to participate,
it lands in my lap.

So here I am this night . . . running again, flanked
by more Kevlar than anyone should ever have to
wear. You are hunting high-threat scumbags around
the globe. Like Indiana Jones, bounty hunter, you
appear. You are asleep in a military bed, surrounded
by guns and planes and missiles, safe as bug in a
rug after three whole weeks of being anything but.
I have heard two nights of extreme, primal panic in
the dark marred by foreign languages and threats of
a terminal nature. This kind I have felt before; most
people don't even know it exists. Thank God for them
and blissful ignorance. They are the kind of happy
that allows a normal life without any real mental
maintenance or malady. They watch the news and *30
Rock*, and everything is just fine. They take safety for
granted. They are clueless. They think it just happens.
Kumbaya. Lucky them.

Meanwhile, I'm tied to the other end of a phone.
Grasping at every breath like straws, not wanting
to let you go out of complete and utter fear.
Pacing wide-eyed and sheet-white and brain-dead,
waiting for that communiqué to let me know that

everyone—especially you—are in one piece, safe and sound, the way all of you were when you were sent off in love and innocence by your families.

I have communicated with you those nights, praying that I could pull you through alive and intact. I helped make you clear and able to focus. It's vain of me to think of myself as so important to you, but you tell me that I am. I'm young and stupid enough to believe what I hear. You told me that I am and have been your lifeline, pulling you through, and that you know you couldn't have done it without me helping you.

I breathe hard and cry when no one's looking or listening and hope that my senses don't fail me. That I always can steer and make people hear me when they need to. I get to "hear you" by text inside a jet, being whisked away like a Faberge egg. Just so you know, one of my nicknames was Faberge, because of an ex-boyfriend. One of his ex-girlfriends met me and assumed I was a vacant—beautiful thing and that was that. She nicknamed me. Now it's function is apparent. Just a typical day in my world and not surprisingly in yours as well. The precious egg head that carries all of the world in her/his insides. No one has any idea of what's in there. They thought it was all about the luscious cover that glistens in the sunlight. But they never know about the inside, which has everything to do with being able to see in the dark. Here's hoping you've become adept with your night-vision glasses. I have a feeling you're going to need them.

I pray the people around you know what they are doing and are infallible. I cannot afford for them not to be. There are people I know and love, the most precious cargo at stake. I have been grateful for your group and others for your safety for years, even before I met you. I understand what this means; you don't need to tell me. No one is allowed to anyway. I know this. I understand before it happens. I know it before it goes down. It is exhausting to be so aware of a world you cannot see. That aside . . . what were the chances? That we would meet and that we would get out? This time—any time?

Months ago, you told me that I stepped through a dark portal and that there was no going back, ever. The funny part was that you thought I didn't know and that you had to tell me. Funnier still, was that you were the one, along with your team, that came through a numinous hole. It was like *Alice Through the Looking Glass*, but no one had to take a pill.

There are questions I ask myself every day, every time it dawns on me. I dare not ask you, scared that there might be a real statistic, a number, a study, or any other input that tells me that I'm correct. I don't want to be. I almost never want to be.

I found the hotel. It dropped into my lap like rain. It had a history. Only we didn't. I got an e-mail, followed a banner ad, did the research, and before long, we were set. I was going to Washington, and amazingly so were you, after having returned from Europe, the Middle East, and other points in the Med and the Ottoman Empire. You were whole, which was unbelievable after the three weeks we had just been through in the dark on the phone in more time zones than you could count. You continued to lie, as you were taught to. To protect, to save, to serve all the things that you had come into contact with up to this point in your life.

The group doesn't hand you a manual on how to deal with a civilian that thinks like a high-level operative, has the skill set to back it up, and can move situations with her mind.

You let me know that you missed me while you were abroad working. You let me know that you never ached for anyone the way you ached for me. But that came much later. More than anything, you let me know that you were intrigued, confused, scared, and falling in love. Not that you recognized what that was, because outside of your children, you had absolutely no idea what that felt like.

Females, to so many of the guys in the groups, are basically the enemy. They are used for sex as long as they are willing. They are collateral damage. You were not prepared for someone who could treat you like a sex symbol and let you know that you were beloved at the same time.

It was called love, and slowly he got the message, starting on that hot summer day in the hotel that would become their place. A day with the curtains pulled that turned into night. She could share the driver's seat and would care for him and not hurt him. Unlike most girls that wanted to get near him, she was never a threat. He could not trace the calls for the life of him; she was so absolutely intriguing. He had never been in a place so safe, and he couldn't decide which need was greater, to merge physically with this thing, or to curl up in a ball on its lap and sleep like he had never slept since he was born. She had an agenda. She already knew that she needed and wanted both. She had hoped that he would come along for the whole ride. She was head over heels in love with this man and had wanted to be with him physically, mentally, and emotionally since the first ten minutes in his presence.

She fell for him with complete devotion and would not leave him while he was in the Med. She knew what she could do for him and did it when he needed it from across the world before he knew what hit him. She kept him steady and straight, and he felt newfound power and clarity and energy and had no idea why. He was in a terrible situation in ten different places in less than two weeks, running for his life. People were trying to sabotage and kill him at every turn.

She told her mother, who knew her intimately, that this man was speaking to her while traveling like others had done before. That this man needed her, and she could not be dragged from his side no matter what. That she knew the difference between his survival and his demise and that she was standing in the way of point-blank range and would not allow it to happen. Her mother was only taken aback by the profundity and the matter-of-fact delivery, as if this happens every day.

Grace had guarded her daughter ad nauseam for her entire life, knowing what she was capable of. She did so quietly, never speaking about it except to tell her to not tell anyone, and never making her feel like a freak because she could do things that other people could not. The child had always been a numinous, and her mother was afraid that there would be a knock at the door and the feds would come and take the baby away, cut her up into tiny pieces, trying to figure out why her wiring allowed her to know things and places and times and people that normal people were not supposed to know.

Aria was a freak, but she had always been one, so with no other frame of reference, she was good. No mental malady, and she had serious backbone. Adversity coupled with character had made Aria strong. So when she met her physical, mental, and emotional match, she latched on in a way she didn't recognize previously. There was nothing else to do other than to show him. Defend him, preserve him, protect him, empower him, align him with all the power that she could move to ensure that his safety and best intentions for the world were never ever messed with. It was plain and simple, just like her; her M.O. never changed from the time she was a child. She realized that his had never either. It bonded them. A clear vision of morality, of whatever it took, whenever and wherever. Things he was taught by the company and by his tight-knit family from the time he was little. Things that she knew in her cells from the universe. They were children in adult bodies acting like adults, unlike most of the world, which seemed to be caught in a perpetual state of teenage self-absorption and angst. Adults, willing to step up and make nasty, difficult, and unpopular decisions and stand by them. People not giving a damn what anyone thought or how much people liked them or what the latest opinion poll said.

Responsibility, it's a dirty word. People now would tell you that it's mean and cold and unfeeling, and it's not saving the polar bears, and it's not warm and fuzzy. Because it doesn't pet everyone and make everyone feel good about completing something that will have no impact whatsoever. But the fact of the matter is that to make difficult decisions and to be the ones to carry them out is loving—much more so than the warm and fuzzy, which is puddle deep. The difficult path represents real belief and hope for the future and people who come along long after we leave. Slogging through blood and guts now ensures stability later. Self-sacrifice for people you will never know represents the ultimate in respect, honesty, and love. It's not pretty, but it is highly effective and selfless, which is immensely loving. You don't care who gets the credit. You care about the outcome, how you get there, and that you do. It's not surreptitious or underhanded; it just is, period. No one does anything they do because they want to be recognized. In fact, it's not in anyone's best interest to be recognized. It would compromise the process, the job, and safety. And that's not an option. Not today, not ever. That is our world, every day.

Penn always dressed well. He had a penchant for conservative, classic, expensive-looking casual clothing. The kind that almost smelled like money, like so many other men in his profession. Clothing that would allow you to disappear in Washington, allow you to blend. There was a disparity. Some things he would spend money on; he was a total snob. Other things would not even dawn on him. It had nothing to do with money. There was always enough of that when he needed something. It had more to do with the way he was raised and the time he had been raised in. He was a punk kid in the times when everyone else was listening to The Doors and Janice and getting high. He was busy chasing girls, going to school and writing, and running with his friends while he listened to the music. He would rather screw girls, play football, and work out than get high. God forbid you get so obliterated that you couldn't fuck well. That was so much more fun and profitable and laughable. Why would you want to get so messed up that you couldn't take care of the flavor of the week? Priorities, man . . . where are your priorities? He could pretend to fit in just a little bit in DC. Hell, there he was almost cutting edge. Washington was hardly a bastion of the fashion forward or for people with any awareness whatsoever. Given the gay populous, that alone is an oddity.

Washington should be like San Francisco, New York City, or Key West, but it missed the memo saying that gay men are the designated design gods somehow. People in Washington wear their pants too high up, and high waters are commonplace. From a fashion perspective, and a gay one, it's like a terrible accident; you can't look away. It's as if they are "Friends of Noah" instead of "Friends of Dorothy." I would shoot a picture for the paper if I ever saw a fabulous woman walking into a meeting in ruby red slippers instead of comfortable shoes.

In Washington, there are only three groups that are highly divergent, and they try hard—too hard. The call girls and strippers and the Capital Hill Barbies, and all three groups are blowing a congress person, and everyone knows it. Despite all of them throwing themselves at him, he never went in for it. Sure, he'd gone along to the clubs; everyone in DC uses them for meetings like Kleenex. But he always viewed those girls as exactly what they are, salespeople. He didn't date down, or even screw down. Most of the boys did. The boys didn't care were they put it; as long as they got it wet, they were good.

As time went on, Penn's whoring around started to get boring and old. Not that he would ever say this to any of his colleagues. They were single and married, young and older, white and black, and from all over the world, but they all had that one thing in common. They talked about chicks behind closed doors when they got together. The last one, the current one, the wife and her sister, the one in every port. Why they were divorcing their wife. She never ever even knew what they did. They never ever do. It was like the upper-level mob, but the women were dumber. The guys all did it all the time, every day. It was their attempt at male bonding. Keeping the whores and the strippers and the lobbyists and flight attendants busy. They did it. They all did it. But he didn't.

He was raised European and in the South and viewed it as disrespectful. Penn considered these women low end, but he wouldn't treat them poorly. He just wasn't buying what they were selling; he needed and wanted more. He was a true romantic. He still believed that love happened in the world, even though he'd felt that he had made bad choices, and he still had not forgiven himself for it—for the fact that he felt he messed up, and his mom and dad would never live to see how well he'd done, and that he could love someone out there that was capable of really loving him. He finally felt that he deserved it. Contrary to what so many people had surmised, he was deep, passionate, and a soft touch. A contradiction to the job he did every day.

No one knew except her. She knew. She knew about him and about his life from the first moment she laid eyes on him, and he knew it. It scared the crap out of him every single day.

Penn couldn't put his finger on what was so horrifying that very first day or week. He just jumped on that plane to the Med with a picture of a girl in his mind's eye. Just like the piece of the mirror that Kay from the *Snow Queen* got in his eye in the Hans Christen Anderson fairytale, it changed his point of view, and things would never be the same. She started to talk to him while he was in the Med, after many days of doing most of the listening. With every statement, he dissected every word and wrote them down. This of course didn't take into account the number of people in the big room that were listening live by satellite, virtually guaranteeing that everyone on the team would know about the strangeness of this interaction after a short time. That they would be a topic of conversation in the covert marble halls, with only high-level clearance. She was not even bothering to think about the inevitable quite yet. She had been avoiding being drafted or participating with the group for a few years now and was quite proud that she had managed to stay out of the web this long, knowing she would get no support from her family and would be sent to some far-flung address abroad. It was just never talked about. When friends and family are highly involved, it just sort of is. You never really think or know anything different.

So Aria had the beginnings of a life, and it was truly strange and colorful, and then she met an unlikely compatriot who stole her heart, and then she went to get her gun to cover him. Sounds laughable, but it's true. This was a pretty strong reaction for someone who had never defended anyone who wasn't a blood relative before. She had already made the decision during those days in the Med. That she would defend his children or anyone else that he loved—because she loved him. Her devotion and love were not things that were easily given. People did not just pass through her life; she felt it. Using people like plastic bags was never something that worked for her.

The women always threw themselves at him. Everywhere he went, it was a lot to deal with for her; it was always difficult. Chicks promised to throw their legs in the air. She had seen and heard so many plays, and e-mails with him saying, *I'm seeing someone—no thanks.* The women would even do it in front of her, as if she was invisible or wouldn't get it, as if she was not sitting right there. They just keep bugging him, blowing "girl rules" to hell. He wondered for a while why she didn't like women very much, and then he finally understood their typical pattern of behavior; he got it. Because of the way she looked, women treated her terribly. It became annoying to him, because Aria was good to everyone. She had no agenda, and to constantly watch her being treated poorly hurt him.

Aria let him know about women: you could not trust them, at all.

Once she became an adult, she understood. It had been done to her, and it was peasant behavior and not something she would ever take part in. She was taught not to. If men tried to get away with what women do by nature, they would all kill each other every day and never have a single friend. She had the opposite problem, and it was hard for him to picture. Unique and intelligent and not willing to play the "Bambi, the Stupid Bimbo Game," men were intimidated. The less intelligent specimens would not even begin to approach her. Only while drunk did men seem to have the fortitude to let the fur fly. Liquid bravery was the rule of the day. Men tended to make asses of themselves in her presence. At least he and she had that in common, they agreed.

From her point of view, this was sad and laughable and weak. Men of all ages would be shot down if they came in too close at range, as she was rarely impressed. She was never the type that got asked to the eighth-grade dance. She was the type the teacher wanted to hit on, and did. Doing everything they could to get in her pants. She wondered why the boys never asked her out and why the girls were so evil to her and her mother from the day she was born. Slowly, she figured it out, and it was disturbing how mean people were. Aria had only ever had a string of unsatisfying relationships, with the guys realizing what they lost and telling her she was the best sex they ever had and would she please come back and please marry them. But she was over it. She never wanted any of it. A completely different M.O. than just about any breathing female. She was kind to people and warm once she was in a relationship, and she gave more than anyone else she knew. There was always a danger there. Loving someone too much, being treated poorly because of always being the giver, never the taker. There had been only a couple of people that protected her in the way that she so desperately needed, so it wasn't something that she took for granted. She still wasn't used to being given to; it was foreign to her.

Aria met Penn, and suddenly she thought about things she had never wanted before. She looked at families when they were out together, and she looked at couples—young, married, happy people and older, happy, married people—and wondered how they did it. Wondered why it was them and not her. Her and this specific man sitting across from her. She could no longer survive without the scent of him on her clothes.

Chapter Three

She knew what he did and had no problem with any of it. She could do it herself. She was a hard ass. At least that's what people thought she was, because the people who knew her well understood that she could do that job and sleep like a baby at night, just like he did. The jobs that no one else wanted to do. The forward movement, the attention to detail, a specific M.O. The gathering of information and the occasional assassination of someone, anyone, even a world leader when necessary to save a larger group of people. To save all the kids at soccer games, and kids having their first beer or sex or baby. So that people would be around to do good for the world. To make sure that they actually got the option. She knew all of it. That he killed people for a living. Only when they needed killing. Sometimes people do.

Sometimes people just need to get kicked out of the gene pool. When they took the option of peeing in the pool, it was unacceptable, no matter what the reason was—because everyone has to swim in the water. This was an issue that they agreed on to the extreme. These were some of the uncomfortable adult decisions that small, elite groups of people around the globe were saddled with making daily. The kinds of things that the teenagers running around shooting their mouths off about in the media. They think they have the real input, but there are too many pieces in motion, and they don't have the real details.

They are Michael Moores and Oliver Stones. They have no idea that there are groups planning their and their children's and their dogs' demise daily. They rebuke the system that has provided for their families. They think they are going to sit around a tent and make smores over a fire, sing songs, and blog about their graham crackers and pop tarts, but they aren't. The people that they are dealing with are survivalists with nothing to lose, and they don't eat fucking smores or give a shit. Of course when their sister's train blows up on her way to her *Times* internship, they will be the first person to lawyer up and sue the city and say, "Why me?"

As for him and the matter of survival, he was built big. In all her interactions, she had seen only one other specimen that was so physically large. She never liked or even looked at men like that before, but now he did it for her. He made her feel safe.

One day in a hotel in Washington that was crawling with alphabet agents of every kind, she was sitting in the basement, in a corner, in a chair after a crazy fire drill for no reason. He, the specimen, was on the way to the bathroom, and she noticed him right away because he was another freak like her man, and this was something that you did not see every day. She could tell that he was not smart like her man. The clone was painfully aware of her, but she never gave him the time of day. For Aria, the grey matter was everything and it was non-negotiable. It was the only thing that kept her around and interested.

Sex, when someone liked it, could be taught. Someone could be built into an effective lover. They could not, however, be taught to be highly intelligent and then have the kinds of conversations that those people have. They could not accumulate time in the field and process it and survive it the way the best and brightest and luckiest did. There was no substitute for pure excellence, and she knew it.

He had been given a number since she had known him. Shortly after they met. She was there when it went down. At that exact moment, they knew where she was, what they were doing, and they were already watching her anyway. They knew that she knew, and apparently they were okay with it, surprisingly. She had already been told that her credibility had been widely established. That was agency hierarchy BS for "Carry on, we're okay with you, we know you're a good person, and we have every intention of tapping you when we need to. Don't be alarmed."

She was well aware of the fact that she had been used as a diversion somewhere in the beginning, and then things went horribly wrong. They started to care about her. Her openness and fearless devotion to the man she loved was measurable, palpable. It affected people and things at the agency, and things that were supposed to happen didn't. He was supposed to attend events with her as a beautiful distraction on his arm, providing him and her and the group with a more well-supported cover and a serious illusion, but those were suddenly called off.

People that he had been told were okay to trust, she told everyone in the big room were not okay. This did not make them happy. The fact of the matter was she was right, and they were wrong, and it was uncomfortable to say the least. Things proved to be worse than that on many occasions, as she was almost always right. And when this happened, and everyone could see proof of her abilities, things were definitely not okay.

Aria became an asset to the asset, and this was a new position for everyone at the party, and nobody felt like dancing. She always used to say to Penn, when they were alone and then when their life was on display

there in the big room, that he had to come home safely
to her because "he owed her a dance." After a while,
they just began to speak normally while he was in the
field and on the air because they didn't care anymore.
It was bullshit to play charades anyway. It got to the
point where they would have had phone sex from
the field from far-flung foxholes in Karachi and Paris
hotels, just to make it reverberate around Langley in
the big room in stereo. They took great pleasure in
making even the most callous operative blush like an
eleven-year-old. That was always a nice distraction
when his ass was on the line in some foreign, sandy
shithole with the cockroaches breathing down his
neck.

So until they could be together permanently, their life
took place in hotels. Hotels all over the world were
viewed as home and had come to represent happiness,
normalcy, comfort, and safety. Of course they weren't
really any of those things, and in the back of their
minds, sadly they knew it. They suppressed it, the
sadness of the situation, until they could make it
different.

Anyone else whose lives were normal and boring would
have thought that it was wildly exciting, sexy, and
romantic. But what this high-powered couple wanted
more than anything in the world was a break. In a
safe place where no one on the planet would know

they were there, where there was no GPS, where the phone would not ring, and where the only people with weapons and a license to use them effectively were them. They wanted it, longed for it, prayed for it, talked about it. They were doing everything they could to make it a reality sooner rather than later. They were ready to live on government property, together in a house, if everyone agreed to leave them the fuck alone for a few weeks.

There had been more than a few physical maladies accumulated in his personal life, and in the field in the past year, and Penn had been given almost no down time to have multiple surgeries and repairs to his body. He had been dispatched to multiple hostile third-world and other situations while trying to recover. This gave Aria an ulcer, of course, and her newfound relationship with her digestive tract was legendary. Penn's body quickly followed suit. They hated being separated. They did not play well apart, the twins. Both ends of both of their bodies were broken at different and similar times in various time zones on the same days and nights. The discussion of reverse peristalsis and irritable bowel syndrome became commonplace and laughable. It became part of the deal.

Pregnancy scares were always timely, and her period had become the topic of conversation on many levels.

Aria had migraines since age twelve, but now with the new level of stress from their life together and apart, when they came on, they were incapacitating. They always seemed to send Penn out into the most disturbing situations as she was getting her period, and she was exhausted without fail. This was significant, because the power that she used to affect his situations needed a great deal of raw biological energy and concentration from her physically and mentally, and the blood loss on such a tiny human was measurable. She didn't even weigh enough to be able to donate blood. She would get exhausted, and it was harder for her to concentrate and to be there for him, to tune in and see what he saw and feel what he felt.

Aria felt guilty when she wasn't 100 percent on, and she would get violently angry at the group for sending him anywhere when she was compromised. She was convinced that they did it on purpose, and she wished they would stop. She always knew about the dangers before he was in trouble. The details in her mind's eye were staggering, and they constantly blew his mind. They got to the point where they would take notes and compare notes down to the minutes after the ops, and it was always more than a little horrifying how deadly accurate—down to the minute—she was about his state of affairs. As if she was standing in the room many times. From all the way across the world. From his point of view. With no details and no contact or input. She was the human Garmin. It still unnerved him, even after a year. After a while, he came to accept that he was in love with someone that no one was built to understand, except the few others that roamed the planet and had similar capabilities. It was a bankable commodity, and he was okay with it, finally.

It took a while to identify issues like this and others. There were specific people who dealt with the problems that were unique to life inside, outside, and adjacent to the agency and any and all the alphabet agencies. It was a crazy life and not one that anyone could be expected to cope with on their own. Aria was acutely aware of this. Sometimes you need a little help, to blow off some steam, and spending it with someone you consider a friend and you can trust is vastly superior to going full postal and doing something in life or in the field that's hard to undo. It's not like you can speak to anyone on the outside about anything an way. For starters, they would think you were bat-shit crazy. Then if they did ever believe that you were for real, one of two things would ensue.

They would either tell their colleagues and chat about how to deal with it from a clinical perspective, and then you would have a group that knew about your opps. Or they would think you were a dangerous psychopath and call the cops. That would be even worse, because then papers would be filed, pictures would be taken, and covers would be blown. With that in mind, there was a shrink that they found in order to help them cope.

She asked for help. She started the relationship to deal with the extreme stress, and after many months, she pulled Penn in. Doc Minor became family. He was a safe place in an unsafe situation. The Doc was wonderful and elflike and open and pure. He was such an anomaly in the group in so many ways. He was relaxed and open and figured her out immediately. They became fast friends, first she and he, and then the three of them. When it was time to do any kind of evaluation, he was the guy from the very beginning. The Doc was right there, and he knew everybody's function. He was good at it.

It became impossible for them to have these kinds of relationships outside the group after a while. At some point, you just know too much crazy stuff, and it has to be kept in check. Downloaded as it were, but kept in a safe and controlled environment with air-conditioning and motion sensors to make everyone happy, and to keep it cool. This is what Doc's first function was, climate-controlled, safe, hand-carried storage. She planned it. She was just like her man, always ahead of the curve.

Penn and Aria both had an anger management problem and a high boiling point. When they got there, it would get loud and confrontational, but not with each other. They came to count on each other to calm the other down. This first reared its head in Washington. Aria shot him a "stop it, baby" look. Penn was overreacting because he was upset about something else that had happened to her moments before. It had absolutely nothing to do with the dumb girl behind the desk. She was just some bitch in the way. Aria had never seen him display it before, but she knew it was there that first day in NYC. He just had never tipped his hand before that Washington day, and it would be months before she returned the favor.

Chapter Four

Penn woke up in a cold sweat again. Considering where he was, you would think that it would finally be getting cooler, and of course he wasn't on the ground floor in this hotel. Never on the ground floor, ever—unless it was a setup, with home-court advantage and friends. This was nobody's home court.

It was the middle of the night, and he was awake again. He'd been dreaming about home and hearth and what life would be like with her, and it jarred him more than the shithole he'd been sent to for at least a week. Karachi was not his favorite place. For terrorists, though, all things must pass through Pakistan. It's like a terrorist's Disneyland.

Penn was good. He was so good that he could tell you about people walking down the street, their region of the world, even if they were in Ohio. He described them as having big red arrows over their heads, as if there were signs telling what country and region they hailed from. Like bubbles in comic strips, so patiently clear. These were not things that he was taught; these were things he learned because of time-tested blood and sweat on the ground, up to his ass in survival.

When we catch a terrorist, we find creative ways to extract information. When someone breaks, they tell you all sorts of valuable Intel about their movements—who does what, where, and with whom. The one thing you can always count on is that there will always, and I mean always, be a floor bob of the head to Karachi and/or Islamabad and they'll talk about it like they speak about martyrdom—psychotically, lovingly, glowingly. "Gee, Hamid, now that you've been charged with your orders for eternity, what are you going to do?" "I'm going to Disneyland . . . I mean Pakistan!" Pakistan is like Wal-Mart for terrorists, one-stop shopping. They don't care where the shit comes from; there's always a buyer and a seller, and everyone is willing to undercut anyone from anywhere. They all run through the turnstiles, knowing that it will be easy and that everyone will be at the party. No one ever guards the door or mans the velvet rope or checks the invites or the list. There's not even a doorman to be paid off; that would be Saudi Arabia. As crappy as the setup is, this makes Pakistan spy central on any given day. A mix of locals, good guys, extreme bad guys, and worse bad guys passing through from all over. It's a shithole, in a shit storm, in the middle of a sandstorm, with lousy food and a bad attitude. Welcome to Pakistan, enjoy your stay. No wonder so many people are pissed off and are trying to leave any way they can. It's like Tijuana on crack times ten.

To attempt to blend in as a white or black guy is not an easy trick. Taller, heavier, healthier, and whiter makes for being easily marked on the street. A big no-no. The only time this is a positive thing is when you run across a friendly, one of ours or an Israeli. In those situations, it will save your red, white, and blue, American ass. Of course, agents have to be judged on a case-by-case basis, and you can find good people anywhere. They exist all over in all countries. They are all colors and religions, and they are all ages. Sometimes they're in the places you would least expect. Sometimes the worst ones and the people you cannot trust are your own.

Just look at that fool down at Ft. Hood. Political correctness was responsible for many deaths, and that guy never should have been in the position to do such harm. Even after tipping his hand months before on multiple occasions in front of many people, he was promoted to major. Sent to college to take courses in his chosen faith and radical behavior. What's the deal with that? Exactly who the hell was minding the store here? Not to mention he was caring for stressed people coming and going from the field. A place he had never even been. He never should have been in his position, period. They should have canned him the minute that he showed he was mentally unstable. It was entirely because they were worried about how it looked because of his ethnic background.

The White House just needs to lead, and leave the alphabet agencies that risk their lives every day the hell alone, period—so that we are not sending mixed messages. Once again, people need to be judged on a case-by-case basis. Profiling is not bad thing; even if people do not like it, it works. Boo frickin hoo—deal with it, America. Do you understand the way the rest of the world really works? You believe the news, and you don't have the real information, and you're not going to get it anytime soon. Most of you could not handle it anyway. Hell, right now, 1600 can't handle it, so don't feel too badly. There are at last count, twelve families that have been robbed of vital members of their clan because someone was worried about how it would look and what everyone would think if someone cried wolf. That is so much like a third-grader. What if they don't like me? Whine. Who gives a damn? Do you think those people who died gave a shit who liked them? Hell no, they would rather be alive. But just like the selfish person who gets behind the wheel high or drunk, he's alive in a hospital bed, while valuable beings, loving people, good people met their maker at his evil hand.

This discovery of good people in different situations had of course become readily apparent to Penn more than once over twenty years. And he has worked with groups of people from many countries who have surprisingly not let him down. Despite terrible circumstances, they have done their jobs and risen to the occasion.

Being able to speak some semblance of Arabic has also helped a lot, given the circumstances. Pakistan is a place that you go to knowing there will be at least one group or person whose main objective is to kill you. Your job is to do the same to them and not be on the receiving end. Plain and simple. Then your job is to get out, preferably the way you came in, so that the illusion is complete and you can one day return to do something similar. However, the people chasing you while on your way to successfully complete this operation are not convinced that letting you get through customs and onto that plane is such a great idea. They had other plans for your day and will now probably lose their hands and/or heads to their superiors because they screwed up and let you get away, again. No wonder they hate you.

There were already some countries that were off-limits to Penn. They would be left for others to tend to because they were just too dangerous for him to ever go back to. He would be a marked man the minute he cleared customs. In fact, he would never even see the outside of the airport; it was that bad. But no one knew, and surely civilians that were home snug as a bug in rug back in the States never got the real memo, the one explaining what really went on while they went through the drive-thru getting their designer coffee and *New York Times*. Penn was over it, waking up in Karachi after a few hours of sleep. He was due at his first meeting within a couple of hours, and he had to get up, get a shower, find food and potable water, and check in with a secure up link, all before lunch. It was going to be a full and long day, and God only knew what it would bring.

Even with all the prep and all the pre-field briefs, years of experience had shown him that being a spy and being a successful trial lawyer were close bedfellows. No matter how much you did, how much you prepared, everything was always more complex and always got out of control at the absolute worst and most compromising time. Then you had to pull rabbits out of your ass in a foreign, hostile land and make it work at all costs, or you would not be going home to see your kids. Point-blank range. That was where the problems always surfaced, at point-blank range. There was no pussy-footing around. It was never pretty, and people regularly made an unscheduled exits. It was always big and crucial, and you're far from home and quite fucked, so you had better be connected, confident, and callous to any anarchy that may ensue because you have to really think on your feet. That ability to think on your feet, and that gnaw in your gut most of the time, is what saves your life in a foreign, third-world shithole. He thanked God for his ability at the cellular level to know the difference. That specific ability had put his happy ass, post op, back in a debriefing situation both home and abroad for many years. Easier said than done—always.

He thought about it while staring at the ceiling, waking up. What makes a great agent and not just simply a good one, a competent one? One who keeps coming back alive? What makes an expert? What were the common qualities. Did he possess any of those qualities? Did the agency have a list with boxes that got ticked off? How many boxes had been checked next to his name? Agggh! There was too much to think about this early, and he needed to find some Evian and brush his teeth and take a piss. He had been too tired when he arrived to even get up to pee. The time difference always killed you for the first few days, and he would be staying up later than he should to call back to the East Coast to talk to her at a time he felt he would not tip his hand. Plus he had to lie

about where he was, and that required the quiet of
the dead of night in Pakistan, and no mosques in
the background blaring their calls to prayer. He had
no clue that she already knew where he was and
what he was doing. He was back in the Middle East,
and his body and soul were none the worse for the
wear, amazingly. It was something neither he nor the
agencies officers could say about most of their agents,
or the lifers at his level. He used to say that he was
good at his job, and to him, he was stating a fact to
make other people feel better. It was never a statement
of ego; it was designed to make other people feel
more comfortable, that's all. It was a highly accurate
statement, and he was convincing himself every time
he uttered it.

As time went on and multiple trips to Pakistan ensued,
Aria became emboldened, because like the terrorists,
she had an end game, his well-being. She knew the
situations would amp up over the many months, and
she began to shoot her mouth off to him in private as
well as in the big room so they would know that she
knew.

Penn had seen so many people come and go and not
come home over the years or just crack up completely,
so he was more than slightly amused that he had been

such a lucky bastard. All of this work through the years had given him many specialties that he would come to be known for around Langley. Penn was like a bird, like a human carrier pigeon on several levels. The ways he managed to move material—both physical things and his mental capacity—was legendary. He was humble and played uninformed almost to a fault. He played the bumbling superman, every man quite literally.

On his last assignment, he carried a gift for her out across the border between his formidably sized testicles. He thought nothing of it. Though he quickly told her, he forgot it upon seeing her at the post-operation rendezvous. He felt terrible that he had left it in his office and wanted to bring it to her next time he saw her. Aria was flattered and was sure that this was absolutely the farthest any human being had ever gone—bringing her a gift from behind enemy lines, carried underneath the balls she worshiped on a regular basis. He loved that about her, that she worshiped him just as much as he worshiped her, and you could tell every time they were within feet of each other. He would tell her that she was like sex on a stick. She knew it; she loved the fact that he got it. She loved the fact that he knew she felt exactly the same way about him. When they were in each other's arms, he was so blissed out he could hardly breathe. The sex was that good, and he had waited his whole life for this kind of relationship with "the whole package," as he liked to call her. He said that their physical relationship was better than porn. That fact alone made him so happy at times he thought he would pop. All this and brains too.

Long before they got involved, he started quizzing her about sex, and slowly she started to answer specific queries. He was surprised and turned on, so much so that he thought—as he was taught to do—she must be lying. But as time went on and they spoke about everything from politics to babies and he got to know her and they finally slept together, he learned that she rarely had the patience to lie, unlike most people. She just didn't bother. She really didn't care what most people thought—not enough to lie. It was a conscious choice. She had bigger balls than most men, hell, than most agents. She was damn near fearless across the board, and that was scary as all get out. Damn her, it was intoxicating. He loved it, and she didn't need him, she wanted him. Needing him like he needed her came much later, and he was grateful when it finally did, when he could feel it. He had never been so scared in his life. Totally out of control, and out of whack.

When the day came that he knew beyond the shadow of a doubt that she loved him, he was never so happy.

He felt whole for the first time since he was a child at home with his family. He truly understood his place in the universe once again, and the clarity was blinding and made him at times feel exhausted and invincible.

Chapter Five

On the beginning of this fieldtrip out, Reagan
Airport was teeming with people and spies and
commuting lobbyists, journalists, Capitol Hill Barbies
and senators, all things Washington. Reagan is under
so much surveillance because of its history that it feels
like a Vegas casino or a cruise ship to all points. Every
God-damned moment is videotaped. The videotape
is videotaped. It's insane. It's like a great agent; it
pretends to miss a trick. The trick is that it never ever
does.

Every once in a while, somewhere in the world, you see
someone that you know, or that you have worked with,
shared moments with, and it's always weird. You're
not allowed to acknowledge him or her or interact,
so there's always that grey area when you come
upon someone. It had happened to him a few times,
sometimes at airports. Sitting at Reagan, waiting to go
anywhere, is fascinating and horrifying. It's a Capitol
Hill Petri dish—biological soup for operatives the world
over.

While buzzing around his hotel room with all this live in his head, he was not aware yet of how much Aria hated certain countries because of knowing how the people are or how the government operated there. She often knew where he would be going before he did. She had site-specific information on how it would go down. She always knew when she had to be scared for him. That was the terrible thing for her, and he knew it months after this first trip. She had broached the topic, and it took real courage on her part, and he knew it. She was acting like an adult because she had seen too much of life so early; she met the challenge head-on.

Penn had tried to break up with her once when he was too overwhelmed, and she didn't walk away when he tried to come back. She took him back when he came to his senses. That was how her Thanksgiving Holiday started. "You're being dumped. I'm freaking out, and I'm going to Pakistan as a chum to try and get killed. Pass the white meat please." She was in Miami Airport, standing over the design of Hurricane Andrew at the time. She was in Miami for that too. The storm clouds always chased her.

She got weak in the knees and wanted to vomit, but she swallowed hard, and the tears came. She felt she would die without him. She came at him with the what ifs, the adult issues, and the problems. She did it out of respect for herself and for him, and for all the children involved, and for everyone that would come after both of them. It was like making a will. That conversation made them uncomfortable, but it had to be done. After all, he said he wanted to spend the rest of his life with her. He wanted to divorce his wife; he was prepping for doing that when he met Aria. He didn't want to live without Aria, and his goal was to marry her—or rather to get her to agree to marry him. He knew that would be a tall order; he thought about it every hour of every day. His life had become a chick flick, and for the first time he didn't mind. This chick was no estrogen-laden bitch monster, she was a superhero with a heart and a soul and big brass ovaries that clanged together when she shimmied her heart-shaped ass across a room, just like his balls. It was a brand-new day. He made sure that the top brass knew it all. Unlike the usual deal, this was not some mind-blowing "POA" Piece Of Ass, and that this girl was in for the haul. She was his touchstone and point of contact for the world, and the only person that truly knew him, and he was grateful that he found her at all. He never thought he would. They were to speak only with Aria.

He would tell her from the field, "If I died right now, I would die a happy man because for the first time in my life, I know who I love and who loves me. I have waited my whole life up to this point for you. I did not think that you existed. I am devastated every day that my mother and father are gone, and that they will never meet or know you. That I had my children with someone else, though I love them very much. I have met the person that I was always supposed to be with, my soul mate." Once Penn arrived at that point, he never looked back and never felt any differently.

She always made it clear to him, long before he felt like this, that she would be the one reaching out to his girls should things go terribly wrong. She would make sure they came to a safe place of love and understanding about the man that they and their mother didn't really know at all. He spent time away from home from the time they were small, defending the world and all the good, peace-loving people, so that by the time they were adults, there might still be a world for them to participate in. Penn would have liked to have been at home more, as he was a loving Daddy. He just had very important work to do with two full-time gigs, and a wife he never got along very well with, but she was a great mom.

Sadly, they were better apart than together. Since they had already made the pact to stay together for the children, it was just better that way. When he was out, even though he was often under threat, he had a great deal of time to think. He flew a lot, took many types of transportation, and was alone often. This time was useful on many levels. His self-awareness and internal knowledge would reach new highs over the next year. What he wanted, what he didn't want, and why. How to change what he didn't want. Where his true priorities lay. He let the brass know that if anything happened to him, they would be lucky if Aria agreed to even be recruited. That would pretty much be the only thing that might garner a yes on her part.

Penn was learning about Aria. She had already fed him and them so much valuable information—more than he had time to follow up on in the coming year. So he just kicked it up the ladder. Aria was valid, and everyone was beginning to know it. He just kept making them more and more aware. They were fusing things to make the process even more effective, and they were coming to him and her whether they liked it or not. They were the most effective and unique unit on the planet with capabilities together that no one else in their position had, and the Company knew it. The group slowly started to get the message and decided it would better to saddle this horse and take the reins than to have no control at all.

He had managed his uplink with little difficultly after climbing out of the shower, and he hoped that this would be the measure of the day. Getting last-minute phone calls from Langley always perked up his ears. At least today there would only be phone calls to one place, and he would not have to call and tease his "Mama Bear." Mama Bear is what Penn called his "den mother" for his unit that kept tabs on him the world over, so that more than one person of trust knew his movements. He checked in often and would get reprimanded when he did not. The group was very serious about the safety of their agents/assets. When he was on an op, all of those groups held hands immediately, so Mama Bear would not have the pleasure of getting grief from her favorite agent today. Secretly, Penn missed talking to his Mama Bear. It had been a ritual for many years, and to change the rhythm was strange. Today had not been harsh or unexpected from his point of view—just some last-minute operational details and updates. Thank God for small favors. He had too much on his mind already and woke up after only three hours of sleep in Pakistan.

The smell was like a camel's ass; it was hideous. The noise of the people just functioning. Smog hung over the city constantly, so that between that and the dust, you could never stay clean for even half the day. The terrible smell of the people everywhere. The in-your-face poverty was oppressive. The worst were the children—orphans starving, neglected, and abused. The way the men treated the women as chattel, and how Islam condoned it, every bit.

He couldn't wait to get the fuck out. Penn was already counting the minutes, hoping the operation would go perfectly so he could get on a plane to the next location as soon as possible. If he ended up in a place where Islam was not the rule of the day, it would be easier to call the girl, even if someone was chasing his ass. The goddamn mosque announcements were loud as all hell, and he couldn't risk having that shit in the background of a casual phone call to someone having a normal day. She was smart, really smart, and she would have gotten it and traced it by sound and figured it all out—and that he could not afford. Plus Langley would have been pissed at his carelessness. So that was it. Today was going to be text-message heavy, no calls, "lalalalllla" over the loud speakers kind of day. Penn was stuck in Pakistan—oh joy.

Off to his first meeting, hitting the street. Trying to blend in, walking slumped to appear shorter and less physically formidable. Drab colors, cheaper clothes than he liked. Work clothes. Dark clothes are always best; they travel well and don't show dirt in dusty places. Most of all, dark clothes don't show blood, in case you get any on you. You know that's going to come in handy, because someone almost always gets shot. More often than not, it's what you're there to do. It's not like there's water everywhere and you're likely to find a spy standing in his drawers and socks in someone's hotel room washing the blood out of his shirt, bobbing his head to his iPod and singing "I Will Survive." Never gonna happen. But you can't really be tooling around Karachi or Islamabad in a blood-splattered shirt. Don't wear or take anything you love, or you will be liberated of it. It's always a cheap throwaway. There are many more of them than you, so you don't invite trouble. In Islamabad or Karachi, trouble finds you with no map needed. So blend, blend, blend as much as possible. It's always a crapshoot which side wants to have you there less. Do you want to be there even less than they want you there? It's like the guy who's taking everyone's money and winning at poker. The entire time that guy is there, you're plotting how to take your money back. But you don't want him to leave until you have your money back.

That's why everyone gets drunk—because they know they're not getting their money back. The chances are slim. Same as why everyone joins the jihad. Life sucks in Pakistan for most poverty-stricken men, and they will try to get out any way they can—even if they have to escape to the afterlife in order to get laid by some chick who would never have blown them in this life. So, as a rule, they don't have a lot to lose, and they have a bad attitude. Some imam comes along and tells them that in their next life their lot will be different. Damn, where do I sign up? Who do I have to kill? That big white guy with a big dick and a hot girlfriend and a nice car? Cool, I can do that. That Allah is one cool dude. Bonus.

Aria thought the whole thing was insane, but she would never tell him until months later. She was sweating badly. He was in the Med and multiple other locations, and he was being threatened. She of course was aware of this, and he was running for his life. This was the first time they were on the phone when the shit hit the fan. It would be their first fieldtrip together. She knew he was in dire straits and counting on her. But Aria did not let him know that she got it. She did one thing that could have given her abilities away, but it was still too early on, and he didn't have a clue yet. She dropped "the F bomb" live in the big room, via satellite. She was not in the habit of swearing, especially in front of people, and never that word. Hell or damn—sure—but not fuck! She knew he was in trouble one afternoon, and she yelled, "Fuck!" during one of their heated conversations. She wanted him out of there. She was mortified and apologized profusely. It bothered her for months. She told him she knew that everyone and their mother had heard her. She was so embarrassed she wanted to crawl into a hole. Penn told her what she already knew, that they were used to it. "Hell, you should hear us. Everyone knows, and they're used to it—it's okay." She joked, "I guess no one ever says 'oh gee' on a black box before a crash; they swear like sailors under great duress. It's human nature." The group was quite familiar with behavior like that, but still it horrified her.

Sitting in a restaurant wasn't a foreign function to him and neither was ordering Middle Eastern food. What was foreign was waiting in a hostile country, watching the door. He placed himself in the power position in the room where he could see everything that he needed to, the ways out of the building, the location of the bathroom, and its windows. He was as relaxed as bait could be. He was waiting, pretending to be something that he was not, and following in someone else's footsteps to gather information. Months from now, the valuable Intel he managed to gather on this trip would give the agency the input they needed for the next go around, and the ability to make some semblance of amends for wrongs that had been done to others. He did not know that yet, but he would. Often during specific operations that are set into motion for one cause or to further one agenda, it works out that agents often scratch the back of another need that is more immediate and critical in nature. In other words, while someone in the field is out doing their job, they often trip over something very valuable. "Happy accidents" like that happen all the time, and Intel agencies could not be so effective without them. Contrary to what Washington currently supports or the news organizations report, there is no substitute for Intel, people on the ground, and long-term investment in loyal locals. The good agents that peace-loving, democratic nations interject regularly to hotspots around the world are amongst the bravest, most valuable, selfless beings on the planet. They often do not get out alive. There are, in fact, very few old agents. It is a very exclusive, small club that you cannot ever admit you were a part of. Very few people aspire to coming home to their families in pieces in a plastic bag. But to the agents who work in this part of the world, that is a real-world scenario and an everyday reality. It's something that their families will never know. It's something the current administration takes for granted and believes has outlived its usefulness. This is not something that most of the news organizations are ever privy to, and yet it happens quite often. People pay the ultimate price often for the nation's benefit, and no one is even allowed to admit they exist. But the teams know that when they sign their lives over to every other decent citizen in the world, and they do it anyway. They make real-time decisions to preserve life, limb, and safety for all the people of the world. The world not blowing itself up is a positive thing. Things not falling into the wrong hands is a positive thing. Most of what the agencies do are things along these lines. Very little is actually punishment for past deeds, though most involved wish it was a bigger part of it.

The good guys like to win, and when someone who is good is wronged or innocents are wronged, Americans love to step up and level the playing field. Americans love to take care of people. Americans were the underdogs since the beginning, so they can relate to being taken advantage of and underestimated, and they don't like it very much. So Americans changed it with democracy. But it took time and passion and fortitude and leaders and followers. It took everyone having moments of bravery. People around the world now are doing things big and small to oust oppressive, violent, abusive, corrupt regimes, and are looking for guidance and backup and a friend to assure them that they're doing the right thing, sacrificing for their future grandchildren. But as much as our people on the ground like to assist at all levels and revel in watching colleges and hospitals and restaurants spring up in places where they used to spew hate and make weapons, it's difficult. When you're around to see people get to choose their path and not get vilified for it, and when you see them able to pass health, safety, prosperity, a work ethic, and peace onto their children, that is a good day, a very good day indeed. Americans like good days. We've built our whole society on good days, despite people's different backgrounds from all four corners. We make an unwritten agreement to play by those rules. We even wrote some documents about that approach, the most important being the constitution. It's worked well so far. Some of the biggest believers in those documents and the sanctity of them are the guys and girls on the ground. They prove it every single day by putting their selfless backsides on the line, so that all of us can have the quality of life and limb and safety and prosperity that exist in only a few places on the planet. Because many of us take what they do for granted and don't have to worry about the big stuff, we get to have what we consider normal lives.

Chapter Six

Back to Karachi, where he was waiting—waiting to see what would happen, waiting to make contact. Waiting to see what he thought this day might bring. That's the thing about assignments, and especially in this part of the world; they were always such a crapshoot. No matter how well executed they are, no matter how well-intentioned the people or the planning, they get a little funky. Sure, you might get your objectives and then some met, but if you manage to stay alive and afloat and do multiple operations there, the outcome is always the same. Mitigating damage or future damage. There are just so many of them, the jihadists—so many bad guys and so many people that don't care what or who they lose.

Money rules the day, and there are always more bad guys to slow down, interrogate, kill, or track to get to a bigger fish. There are so many groups, splinter groups, and subversive cells that connecting them would be akin to the human genome mapping project. Driving them is a mélange of motivations; if it isn't money, it's hatred of the United States, or nationalistic fervor, or religious zealotry, or just a warped perspective spawned by the poverty that dooms millions of people to a life of misery and despair around the globe. For many of these groups, recruiting young people, even children, is no problem because anything looks better than what this life has dealt them.

Among the first to sign up are the brain-dead people between twelve and seventy-two that are willing to blow themselves to hell. *What a shitty testament to the state of the human condition*, Penn thought every time he ventured into the Sand Box or an East European Ghetto, or a jungle infested with would-be "revolutionaries" hell-bent on targeting the United Sates in one way or another. Fortunately, most don't have the knowledge, the goods, the backing, and the experience to carry out a successful operation, whether it's to pull off another 9/11, infiltrate a government R&D lab, or penetrate the US intelligence community—most being the operative word. But some do. And they are getting better and are damn persistent. Penn and the people in his world were aware of it on every level. The way that America naively allows these people into the country and then shields them with the very laws that were crafted to protect the peace-loving Americans that they seek to destroy, blew his mind every day.

The average person was so out of touch with the reality of the situation worldwide that it baffled those

who saw what was happening. Penn saw it. It tore
at him every day and fed a seething hatred for the
country's enemies and his compulsion to eliminate
them whenever he could. Everyone he knew felt
the same protective urge. The Brits were already so
disappointed with their own past foreign policies that
they had all but begged America to learn from their
careless, naive, fantasy-laden happiness and *kumbaya*
approach. France and some other countries in the EU
had come to the realization that radical Islam was like
a cancer that had to be contained or excised from the
country's social and political fabric. They had been
stepping it up lately, struggling to keep their citizens
safe. That's the reality of control when someone has
malevolent intent; if you don't crush it coming through
the door, you pay for it in bodies one hundred fold
later. By then, it's too late to stop the snowball going
downhill, and all you can do is mitigate damage, which
is then like full-time slavery. The reality of the world is
something that most happy-go-lucky Americans never
acknowledge, and that fact weighed heavily on Penn's
psyche and even seeped into his dreams. He and
other senior operatives often discussed how American
foreign policy had seemingly gotten less influential
with each passing year, garnering less respect around
the globe. Faith in America abroad had slipped, and
so had America's backers. Foreign governments in
countries that were not allies reveled, and they were all

too ready to fill the void, exploiting the weakness, lack of experience, and stomach for reality.

To calm himself and to achieve blessed relief from his angst, he would think about music, sex, foreign policy, his girls, his car. Living a double life was one thing, but Aria was something else. He obsessed over the girl and when they might speak again. Later in the week, when he knew he would be in another location, he thought about the fact that he might have the chance to stop in one of his favorite local restaurants with the proverbial million-dollar view. He wanted her there, sitting across from him, smiling at him while the sun went down, The ruins of the Acropolis silhouetted against the sky in the distance. He pictured her there with him in a little black dress from Paris, a little bit longer than too short to conceal the palm-sized pistol he knew she would have strapped to the inside of what had to be the most delicious thigh he could ever imagine kissing. He had yet to sample the real article, but he hoped to be on his way sooner rather than later. In the meantime, he indulged his wildest fantasies, which would rival anything Larry Flynt or Hugh Heffner could conjure up in their one-track minds.

Penn also thought about his kids. He usually panicked just a bit whenever he got sent out on an extended assignment abroad. As his daughters had gotten older, he reveled in the newfound relationships he was able to have with these newly minted adults. He was a proud father, and growing prouder every year at how the girls were maturing. A new kind of problem was emerging—their growing curiosity about him and the world he inhabited. They had started asking more questions. Because of pop culture, the heightened awareness of his kids, and their own smarts, they were less and less satisfied with his answers. Penn found himself torn between being a parent, wanting them to use their brains to figure it out, and covering his ass as an operative. It was an internal struggle that all the agents faced about their secretive double lives. but it was something the agents never spoke about. Your kids weren't ever supposed to know. Neither was anybody else outside of "The Community" for that matter. And for good reason. It could cost you your life or another agent's, or the life of someone you loved. The first rule of survival in the spook business is guard against leaks, which can be deadly. They would routinely grill case officers and people attached to clandestine operations like bull-dog lawyers doing a cross-examination. No one could afford to be compromised. A few times, the kids had gone "fishing," blowing his privacy and trust like a small kid looking under the bed for Christmas presents. It was wrong, and they knew it, and then they went running to Mommy right away, as soon as they found anything they didn't understand. Fortunately, Mommy didn't either. Not that anything was incriminating or they were able to put the puzzle together.

Hell, Penn had been with the same person more than thirty years, and she still didn't know him at all or get it. This amazed him. It confounded him about most women he had known. The kids did what any normal American kid is taught to do, tell a grown up. Sadly, they already were grown up and should have gone to their dad first. But the couple was already at the point where the relationship was unstable on its best day. He felt guilty. He tried for so long to love her. For so many years, he tried to build with her what he grew up with. Penn wanted that familial intimacy. He craved it and prayed for it, but it never came. Cold and prone to emotional tirades, she rejected him. She also had none of the physical needs Penn had. Trying to salvage the relationship became too draining. It just became too difficult. The years were flying by, and she still didn't know him or really seem to care to. He needed intimacy and warmth and companionship, even if it wasn't real or what he dreamed about. He was ready, willing, and able to sacrifice his life and laid it on the line in two areas. After many years though, he just couldn't do it in the third arena. He wanted to be happy and feel loved. So after a while, he shut down emotionally and spent more time away working because it was just easier that way. They couldn't fight if he wasn't there. It wasn't good for the kids, and he could not bring himself to leave them. So he stayed. They made an unwritten rule like so many couples do—to stay together to raise the children. The girls never knew, and they grew up thinking that everything was fine. Or at least normal. When he was at home, he missed the work, and when he was in the field, he missed the girls.

As they got older, he welcomed the chance to have the kind of relationships with them he had wanted his whole life. He could speak to them as people, not as babies anymore. Putting stock and validity in their exchanges, he loved it. It was precious to him. He was amazed how his drive to protect them had not diminished as they became more self-sufficient. He hoped that they never found the stash of weapons and secret things he kept hidden at home, and he hoped that they never needed to know about Kevlar vests, silencers, and armor-piercing rounds that weren't standard issue in the regular world. He was used to having to having to cover his tracks professionally, but he hated the fact that he had to mask his real identity and purpose in his everyday life. He was really just a goody-goody when push came to shove. For him, deception was more of an effort than a skill that came to him naturally. At heart, he was a choir boy; it's just that his business could get very ugly and usually involved the highest of stakes.

Penn was itching to return to the field, disguised as a high-profile journalist on the world stage, and then at the appointed time, zero in on his real mission. He could embrace any location. Washington, NYC, Paris, Oslo, hell—even LA. He never liked LA, especially the people, but anything was better than here. With the number of Middle Easterners in LA, it could feel like Amaan or Abu Dhabi. But he was hell and gone from Formula One tracks, good architecture, polo mallets, and Hermes bags. He grew up average, an average American. Now he knew the difference, and he was well aware that one side had it all over the other, and there was no doubt about which side had the favor of the gods. It wasn't the current group that was bowing five times a day and hunting his ass.

Chapter Seven

The café he was sitting in was playing a bizarre mix of what could only be described as Middle Eastern, Indian influenced, French techno. The kids seemed to think it was okay, but it was the weirdest shit he had heard in a long time. He would have given his left nut for the familiarity and calming effect of The Beatles, the Beach Boys, Skynyrd, or even Patsy Cline. He wondered what the parents of the kid who composed this musical masterpiece looked like. *Holy hell,* he thought, *where did the two people who gave birth to this kid meet?*

He tried to wrap his head around such trivialities and dissect everyone that was caught up in their own activities around him. He wondered if the grape leaves would taste as good as he remembered—and whether he would have the time to enjoy them; he had left a trail of destruction on the mission he had just completed. He could feel his stomach screaming at him. He always got testy when he was hungry; it takes a lot of calories to move a big body. Since this was a locals-only joint, there was a chance that the fare was still his kind of food—substantial and seasoned just enough to delight his taste buds. He avoided neighborhood cafes; the last thing he needed was a gastrointestinal adventure. All the same, it was a constant risk outside of the United States, and so he usually carried Company-issued antidotes in his pocket. Hell, while on assignment in Indonesia he packed a bottle of Pepto-Bismol in his inside jacket pocket and drank it like it was Kool-Aid. If he was messed up, the only place he would want to be is Israel—amazing doctors there, the next best after NY or Mayo or LA or Washington.

He thought some more about the girl with the gorgeous legs that he couldn't wait to examine up close and personal. He didn't know that she had many friends and had spent time in the Middle East herself or that she had grown up in a Catholic family like he did. The difference was that her family kept an Israeli flag in the closet next to the Red White and Blue, and grasped the delicate balance of power and democracy in the Middle East.

Her dad had spent a great deal of time in France and Italy and North Africa and had a real handle on geopolitics in the region. He started training her as a child. Geography, topographical details, logic, how to care for her body, dialects. He impressed upon her the importance of listening and observing people in their environment, the importance of learning. It never dawned on him that he was building a future operative. Her choices of what to be when she grew up were always different from the typical girl: pilot, pirate, surgeon, spy. She played army with the boys and enjoyed handing boys their asses. She loved tree-forts and hiding in a field with army gear.

As a small child, Aria would get upset at the thought of dead people. For years, she had a recurring, macabre dream involving death, and she was afraid. One day while visiting the graves of her dad's parents, she told him how afraid she was. He took his daughter aside and told her straight out, "Don't ever be afraid of dead folks." She asked him why, and he told her. "Because, baby, they are the only type of person that can never hurt you." It made perfect sense to her that day in the sunshine; she took it to heart, and she never had a problem again. He taught her to be self-sufficient and a lone wolf like him. He taught her that mind and body were uniquely symbiotic. He encouraged her to try everything and to not be fearful, to put no stock in anyone else's opinion except her own, based on her own experience. She learned how to do everything for herself. Penn had no clue about any of this that day when he sat in that restaurant, thinking about Aria, simultaneously trying to stay focused on keep his ass intact, so he could discover once and for all what it felt like to hold this girl in his arms.

He watched the door for the first ripple of the curtain to signal someone's hand on the door. How could he know what the future would bring? He had yet to figure out that he had met his match. But this, like all good things, would come in time, just as tiny seeds become trees in which you can build a house. Aria was only interested in being a tree in which he could build a house. She felt that given what he did professionally, he deserved no less.

Months from now, he would come to know—curled up next to her in any number of beds around the world—an inner peace and warmth that he had never before experienced. He would be peaceful and light whenever they were together. It never mattered where they were or what they were doing, only that they were squirreled in a dimly lit room, together. Curtains drawn, laying around like big cats on the Serengeti, on top of one another, proud, protective, and open. It would become time that belonged only to them, not to the good of the world or any organization in it. They would hunker down to preserve their sanity and the sanctity of their relationship during some very hostile times.

Little did Penn know while he sat dining alone, wary of his surroundings, that Aria was on the other side of the world understanding what was going on with him, secretly losing her mind with worry for him. She could

tell no one about their predicament. One occasion
that summer, while in a store shopping, she had a
moment of emotional nudity in front of a complete
stranger. He had called her after returning to the
safety of a controlled situation. She was so relieved to
hear his voice after an extended blackout period that
the minute the secure sat link connected, she ran to
the side of the store and dropped her purse to dig for
a pen to take notes. Her whispers and body language
alerted a shopper in the nearby greeting card section.
Aria became aware immediately that a middle-aged
lady was stealing glances at her with love and pity. She
burst into tears. Not usually the type to tip her hand,
she suddenly felt naked in public. But she didn't give
a damn; for the first time, she started to wonder what
would happen in their future. Still unbeknownst to
him, she was cabled to him, body and soul, through
the best and worst parts of what he was experiencing
in the field. They were inhabitants of a visceral and
volatile world that would come to be known as their
existence—their physical, intellectual, spiritual, and
emotional playground.

Chapter Eight

Over the next year, she was introduced, albeit very slowly, to a series of situations and people in and around the Company. She introduced him to some people as well. She started relationships with people for him in order to help him at work and to put good guys where they needed to be. The groups had become so cubby-holed and specific to keep everyone safe that it was hard to get alphabet soup groups with recognizable names to work together. It was completely a security issue, nothing else. Everyone she dealt with as a friend, family, or lover was protected and trusted her completely. She always made a point of voicing her true intentions. She would start sentences with, "This is my goal," or "This is what I want, and here's why I'm doing what I'm doing." People had the option to engage and befriend someone or not. If they worked together or had coffee or sex outside of their work, it was their choice, not hers, and she never put pressure on anyone. Aria just had a handle on who would be good together and who would protect each other. They had a way of weeding each other out. She never pulled anyone in that did not have the best of intentions. True patriots only—everyone else need not apply. She cared only about the quality of the character of each person.

Penn was stuck in Pakistan. As much as he loathed being there and wanted to get the hell out, he was going nowhere until he finished his mission. Everything about it sucked. At least he had been there enough times that he knew the basic things that got a person with fewer survival skills killed. Islamabad always feels like you're on another planet, surrounded by alien creatures. Everything is assaulting, every minute of every day. Anyone who says it's a beautiful culture is either stupid or needs to have their head examined. For a Westerner who is used to clean water and air, electricity, a safe food supply, indoor plumbing, religious tolerance, and respect for the female gender, Pakistan like Afghanistan sucks; he had come to the wrong part of the world. There is just no way to get comfortable in Pakistan.

Penn knew the minute he hit the ground running he needed to find water, no easy chore. Fortunately for him, he knew some of the local purveyors. He learned to recognize the local labels that were safe, and so he stockpiled them the entire time that he was there, like a squirrel that stockpiles nuts in multiple hiding places. It wasn't much different when it came to food. He was always scavenging for food. Where he could eat? Where was it safe? Who sat where? Were there locals? Where could he pick up snacks? He had food stockpiled in a safe place and on his person, always the survival stash. Same drill different day. You never come between a big guy and his safe food supply in the third world. He will take you out without blinking twice, and then he will go back to Kansas and take his kids to see Sesame Street on Ice, hug puppies, and make love to some hot blonde wife who can drive a truck, a plane, a stroller, and a tractor. It's all in a day's work for him, no virgins included.

You're looking at a happy man that Jesus, Buddha, and Jewish folks are all just fine with—everyone but Allah. Boo frickin' hoo; he felt so bad. Tough shit. He was there to save people, millions of them the world over. The scumbags that he crossed swords with didn't care who they killed. Their game was destruction on a massive scale. They were equal opportunity offenders. They just didn't give a damn—never have, never will. There was one thing for sure: you can't change people's DNA, and in Pakistan, it is what it is.

What's more, Penn wasn't about to let all the newfound political correctness and diplomatic niceties crowd out common sense. He knew what he was there to do, and he would not let fear of retribution or novices compromise his safety or his mission. Penn had a soft emotional side and had met many little boys with hunger in their bellies that had not been brainwashed. He would have liked to have taken them back to the United States and given them a new life, but it wasn't possible, and it broke his heart. The other reality was that America had to screen at this level. The United States was about the only country in the world that allowed pretty much anyone to come in. Unlike most other civilized nations, Uncle Sam didn't charge for citizenship or require a prescribed level of education. The average American was oblivious to such facts. They were certainly not going to learn this from the popular press. No one seemed more in the dark than the younger generations, and no one was bothering to teach them civics.

For the most part, it was only the lucky kids with European or Asian parents or military kids who spent time or were raised abroad that really knew the score. Most Americans had no grasp of how most of the world really lived. Young people's lack of understanding saddened him a great deal. We kids were by no means perfect, but we had a much better track record than any other group in history. When we put boots on the ground, we always left, and the only ground we asked for was the land to bury our dead. There was a reason an African kid who started with nothing persevered to get a doctorate, and then went to the States and drove a cab, starting at the bottom, leaving his family, wife, and, child, only to bring them three years later when he could manage a decent apartment and wage. The worst thing you can do to a human being is to steal his dreams, and take away his will to achieve and work, giving him everything. People must push in order to have a reason to live. Why do you think scientists tell you not to feed the wild animals? It's imperative that the adult animals teach their young to push and hunt. It's about self-respect and survival. That keeps all animals alive. Surveying the America he loved, Penn saw too many people with entitlement issues. To him, they represented a waste of what could otherwise be productive lives, which he considered the price of admission to the human race.

To be lucky enough to be born into a democratic republic with options and freedoms should not be taken for granted. There's no free lunch, but you get the option to change your lot in life if you work for it. It was a gift, plain and simple. In most places Penn got sent, you never got the option to change your lot, period. He couldn't believe in something for nothing. Everyone he knew had worked way too hard for everything they had. Their payback was time away from their families, and often blood in the service of their country. People who were slackers had no place in their world, and Penn often thought about this as he saw people struggling to survive in various parts of the developing world. It was real struggle, not someone struggling to pay back college loans after graduation from Harvard. Whining made him roll his eyes at mixers in NY or Washington where he often had to meet with some new rocket scientist of a girl. She would flip her hair and bitch about a broken Lexus taillight and a ticket that she got because she was on her cell phone in Jersey. With so many Americans taking their blessings for granted, Penn and some of the other operatives, the guys and girls on the ground, sometimes questioned themselves about why they put their lives on the line time and time again.

In his case, his ability to see the positives had gotten better lately. There was a girl, the girl of his dreams, and he had her and dreams of a future to protect. She didn't take anything for granted and put everyone else first. She wasn't typical head-down and ass-up in twitter. People got her respect because they earned it, and she didn't trade on her looks. She worked her ass off 24/7. He respected the hell out of her. She was as relentless and unstoppable as any confident man he had ever known anywhere. She would march through fire for the right cause, and he knew better than to ever say no to her or dare her to do anything. Penn was a quick study on her personality traits. All the same, he wanted to sleep with her and love her, but he also thought the Company should clone her. He wondered if they were hip to that yet, because if they weren't, he sure as shit wasn't going to tell them. They had enough ideas already they didn't need any help from him. He was protecting her.

All this had happened in a relatively short period of time, so he took a few phone calls. His belly was doing flip-flops, and he ordered a diet Coke while he waited. One of the calls was the embassy. An attaché informed him of a change in meeting place, and he was asked to make a stop very quickly. He sucked down the coke to calm his belly, paid the bill, and left a tip in the local currency. As he walked out onto the street, he was hit by the stench, the noise, the pollution, and the call to prayer.

It was oppressive. He was happy to hide his eyes behind his sunglasses, and he used them to obscure his true intentions. He headed for where he had to make contact with a government mole—a risky but often necessary activity in his trade. It was now his job to get to a park between the restaurant and the embassy and then to get to the embassy by a certain time. At least he could eat while meeting there and do some research on people he was supposed to meet for dinner. He was supposed to meet some operatives with the Pakistani Intelligence service, and he needed to find out whom he could trust. The mole had proven to be a reliable ally on previous forays into this hellhole, and Penn was counting on him more than ever now. He had learned previously that the home office, while usually armed with the latest Intel, sometimes was behind the power curve, and he could not afford any miscalculations.

Penn jumped onto the packed street and hopped into a little peddle-bike pull cart. For short trips on side streets, this mode of transportation often worked better than cabs, and people didn't look twice at them. He had about twelve blocks to walk to the park, and the dilapidated sidewalks were damn near unnavigable. They were packed with people, vendors, carts, and animals. It reminded him of a carnival sideshow. It could at times get more than a little strange.

In NYC, the funniest thing you might see is a bad drag queen in broad daylight, which was enough to send a straight man back to Kansas. But in this part of the world, you could see almost anything, and it could be gut-wrenching: extreme poverty; corpses; women being beaten and stoned; abandoned, starving children wandering the streets like stray dogs and cats. Welcome to Pakistan. Days before, he'd been in London, where he had flown in from Washington, high-profile like a tourist on holiday. He came through with the usual stuff, his clothes for the higher-end functions and all his garb and shoes for the giant litter box. It was quite a contrast—tuxes and slip-ons, pressed shirts, and dress shirts together with throwaway T-shirts, khaki pants, cargo shorts, boots, gym shoes, and Italian sandals. It was like a schizophrenic fashion spread. There was no rhyme or reason to the inners of his luggage unless you knew what he did for a living. There would be a few articles that would need to be swapped out or ditched once he hit the ground, but at least he would have two days in London to rest, eat, and prep.

Heathrow was always comforting—the last little bit of home before all hell broke loose, whatever form hell happened to take at any given time. Good ethnic food, the last familiar things that he could count on, and people that ran pretty much on the same program and had no language barrier. It gave him one less thing to worry about. Not that there were language issues at this point in his career. He understood and spoke most of the languages needed to take care of business at this point. He was very lucky; he was told he had a great ear, thank God. He blew through baggage and customs without a tail and down into the area where there was a team to meet him. He recognized his friendlies and walked out to a black bulletproof sedan. More of the local guys were waiting to see their buddy. The minute he was in the safety of the tinted windows, they pulled away from the curb, and he was handed a leather duffel bag containing some of the tools of his trade. Inside the case was also a sealed envelope with some of the details of this operation, the latest Intel on the situation and breakdown of his schedule for the next thirty-six to forty-eight hours. Now that he was in a safe situation, he took a deep breath and acknowledged his people in the car. Then his mind wandered to back home, on the East Coast, where Aria would be in the middle of her day. He didn't know what she was doing, but he couldn't wait to find out. He shot off a quick text to her right there in front of everyone, and hoped that she would see it and reply.

For all the wonders of technology, it often failed, and sometimes texts, e-mails, and phone calls wouldn't go through. Penn hoped that he would get to make a phone call to her; it was all he could think about, besides getting back to Washington. When he got to his room, he would have to find food and water, get briefed, and check in. Penn knew his comrades would want to monopolize his time as much as possible, just as they were trying to do in the car while he was taking inventory of the contents of his newest black bag. He would still rather do that alone in his room. Back on the East Coast, Penn did not know that Aria was waiting for him. Would he call her today and make her heart fly and stop all at the same time? She wasn't used to feeling like this about anyone, and she certainly wasn't used to feeling completely out of control 24/7.

Chapter Nine

She had been up since the crack of dawn, worrying about him and pretending to work. She made herself busy to distract her from the reason that she could not sleep—waiting to know that he was down and safe. Their relationship was never on twitter and was never done in real time because of security concerns; Langley routinely held messages up, screening them to protect Company operations. There were extended time lags, and messages got lost in cyberspace. Everyone and everything seemed to be constantly changing locations. Langley watched over everything the couple did.

Penn and his companions finally arrived at his hotel room. It became a constant spy game of musical chairs; it had to be. Two of his wingmen checked the room out and swept it for listening devices, while another operative scouted the lobby, the floor, and rest of the building and surrounding area to make sure there was no trouble lurking. Not many people knew what was up with any operation, but everyone understood about certain agents being specific and unique, so Penn was always treated accordingly.

The guys on the ground only got a piece of the pie. That was all they needed anyway. Everything was on a need-to-know basis. The guys were always around but never when or where you would expect it. They disappeared into their jobs, just like Penn. After a few moments, they informed Penn that they would return in about four hours to retrieve him. Now that he was alone, he quickly opened his newest suitcase for the second time and checked it thoroughly, making sure he had everything he needed. Satisfied, he checked in with Langley. Confident that everyone was holding up his or her end, he opened his suitcase, pulled out his toiletry kit, and ditched his clothes. He felt dirty and wanted to shower before trying to reach Aria. Penn also wanted to try to get some sleep, but he wanted to hear her voice, and for a mental image to be the last thing in his head before he nodded off. He cracked open a bottle of Evian from the table and carried it and his toiletry kit into the bathroom. He fired up the shower, set it to steaming hot, and stepped in. He immediately felt human again.

Penn fantasized about having her there with him and making love to her in the shower, wondering if she would be up for anything like he was. He hoped so. He stepped out and dried off. He wrapped himself in a towel and slid between the sheets, grabbing his phone on the way into bed. He wanted to crash for just long enough to be able to string coherent thoughts. He just wanted to have time to speak to her and not be rushed. He got up again to double check the lock on the door and shut off the light. He quickly shot off a text to home base, politely telling them to leave him the fuck alone for a few hours, because he needed sleep. He tried to reach the girl but only got her voicemail. He was disappointed. Shit! He always took it personally when she missed his calls. It was crazy, but he did it anyway. He figured he would try again in a hour or so. He thought about the day they had discussed—when he would return to Washington, and she would come to see him. That day couldn't arrive fast enough. He drifted off to sleep.

He thought about all this while he was in the back of the peddle-bike. Shit, he really was in Pakistan, and it still sucked. He wished he was back in London prepping for meetings and dinners with the U.S. ambassador and other embassy personnel. But sadly, he was definitely still in Pakistan, and it was no longer the beginning of his trip. At least he was almost to his destination.

Penn was nearing the end of three long, hard weeks, and he could hardly wait. In that time, he had taken care of business in seven different countries, and he was still alive. Bonus! Pakistan was the final leg, and soon he would be jetting home, thank God. The peddle-bike pulled to a stop. He paid the driver and got off the contraption. He walked further into the park, met his contact, and got what he needed from him. Then he walked a couple more blocks and was at the embassy. Penn was buzzed into a secure area and checked in again. He was put in a holding lobby until he was greeted by the military attaché and some other folks at a reception. He made the necessary rounds and then sat down, feigning interest in the goings on. Penn knew what he had to do, and it wasn't here. He was just doing what he was told and showing his face. In his job, it was all about appearances. He sat down at a table where his place card was displayed and had a drink. He slipped into a momentary daydream.

He compared this shindig to the embassy parties in London, Mares, Madrid, and all the other places in the world where he had been dispatched. The similarities, the differences, the people, the food, the skullduggery of it all. The other countries and their outposts always intrigued him. Embassy personnel were essentially spooks operating under the guise of foreign-service staff. When they weren't gathering Intel for the home team, they were generally doing their best to fuck things up big time for the bad guys. Sometimes, the support system, when you needed it, felt like a blanket from your very own room. It made you feel like a child, and you were always grateful for it. Penn waited for about ten minutes while everything was taken care of before he was ushered in behind closed doors.

The local consulate tart came in to offer "her services" before he was in front of a group of people. He had been sitting there reflecting on earlier segments in his trip, and he was perturbed. Suzanne, like most of them, was a carnival ride. She was cute, and she knew it. She had flirting down to an art form, and Suzanne hit on any guy on assignment from the United States. Penn barely acknowledged her and completed his business at the embassy.

In London the next day, he boarded a commercial flight bound for Tel Aviv. He was okay with going to Israel. The drill was much the same there, and he had been picking up the op tempo. The second he hit the ground in Tel Aviv, he was aware of the hourglass. He started getting his normal pre-game jitters.

Penn headed straight to one of the electronic intelligence-gathering installations and stayed there. He went to sleep and then woke and called Aria. Too many time zones in too short a period of time. Rest, it was primal need.

The Israelis got it. They understood Americans and how to protect themselves. Penn always slept while he was there. Three hours in a crash pad and then fresh Intel. Some phone calls to the kids back home and a get-together with some of the locals for dinner and drinks. He wanted and needed to do all of it, but all he could think about was the upcoming heavy-duty crap, returning to his quarters to get some sleep, and calling Aria and have more than a three-minute conversation, where he had to lie about what he was up to. Tomorrow he would be sitting in briefings all day, and it would be really important that he was firing on all jets. The following day, there would be a change of venue, and it would be game on. From then on out, there would be no daydreaming. What was coming would not be pretty. Ahead of him were meetings galore with contacts.

Some meetings were arranged by local people on Company payroll, and some were set up by coordinators in the Langley office. Even though he trusted the relationships that were facilitated on his behalf, he was always on guard and viewed them with suspicion. Information was only given on a need-to-know basis, and he never liked being exposed to more people on the ground than was absolutely necessary. The receptions he had to attend, whether they were in Washington, London, Moscow, or Tokyo, always unnerved people in his circle, guys and girls alike. They never appeared nervous, since they were trained not to tip their hand. But everyone was secretly emptying their bladders obsessively before arrival at any function.

Chapter Ten

Conditioning your body to lie is one of most difficult things to accomplish. It takes years to teach a body to lie effectively, and Penn was really good at it. He had been around the embassy for only about twenty minutes when he laid eyes on a new person that came to the party. It was one of Penn's targets, one of the people he was supposed to meet through an intermediary tomorrow. He couldn't believe the size of this guy's balls. He strutted into the room like a cock in a hen house, robes flowing, and he smelled like new money.

Pompous and condescending, he looked down at all the world's "little people." He was from a big family and could make anyone he wanted disappear. Penn couldn't stand such arrogance; he had a visceral reaction. Such self-absorbed people ran contrary to everything he stood for. Penn had tracked him, and he remembered it from a few days earlier, after crossing into Yemen with a friendly from Israel. The encounter had been arranged by a go between. Penn set off in a jalopy into the Sinai Desert with a frickin' Arab covered in baked-on dust and God only knew what else, who smelled like complete shit, but was working for U.S. intelligence. Driving to the middle of the proverbial nowhere, Penn was never so scared. It took more than twenty-four hours, and that whole night in the desert in a piece of shit ramshackle nomadic hut, freezing his balls off, he dared not sleep. It wouldn't be safe to make a fire. That would guarantee a swift capture and a Hefty-bag funeral, eaten by birds of prey somewhere near the Yemenite boarder, with everyone watching from home by satellite. Effectively, that would suck.

He had been following a lead that led them to at least two targets that had a hand in the butchering of a deeply embedded fellow agent. These few assholes had escaped justice, and Penn's best-case scenario was them being sanctioned with extreme prejudice. He was so looking forward to being the lead man in that particular wrap-up. The pitch, the swing, and then being the one to park the ball. Mickey Mantle, Babe Ruth, Jeeter, Jordan, pick your sports hero—Penn wanted to be that guy. It made him so happy he could hardly contain himself. Back in the States, there were loved ones of the agent assassinated that would never know who he really was or that there were allies who took care of his family. Penn thought that if he and his team were able to take care of business, that would be enough. It made everyone feel better to know that the Company always took care of its own and that they were never forgotten.

He would let the appropriate people know that this guy had forced his hand, giving them twenty-four hours advance, and that he would find a way to terminate this asshole with extreme prejudice by early morning. Penn would follow his quarry when he left the party and strike at the most opportune moment. This one was payback for everyone in the agency, and he didn't traverse two additional hellholes and their bullshit to drop the ball now. This was a picture-perfect situation, and this guy was toast. Penn had a new spring in his step. He left the table and quickly went to the bathroom to double check his weapon and send a text to Langley about what had transpired. He knew they would be pleased. This wasn't the first time that being in the right place at the right time had paid off.

Sliding back into the reception, he quickly asked some "pretty thing" to slow dance, watching the man and his entourage the whole time. While he danced, he pretended he was into the girl that he led around the dance floor methodically. The whole time, he was practicing, his partner never the wiser. He watched the scumbag circulate and press the flesh, schmoozing with foreign-service professionals and assorted women as he sipped a small cocktail. His henchmen kept a close eye on their terrorist-friendly meal ticket. Diplomats, spies, and whores—Penn wondered what the difference was between the three types of people.

Having observed for a couple of songs, he needed
to ditch his dance partner for her own safety and
reposition himself. His target was about to exit the
party. He gave her some cash for the bartender's tip
and asked her to go get them drinks while he went
to the men's room. She thought she was going to get
lucky later with some guy from the embassy, so she
obliged him and headed toward the bartender, cash in
hand. He slipped out of the ballroom in what looked
like a casual slide toward the toilet and the common
area outside the banquet room. Then he was gone.
He made his way outside the building and tagged the
car that the "sheik of the week" wedged his fat ass
into. A GPS tracking device had been planted earlier
in the sheik's personal limo, so Penn and his fellow
agents back at Langley could listen to his every word.
Meanwhile, an eye in the sky followed the car to a
compound just outside the city. Once he was sure
of the place where the car stopped, and that it was
staying, he returned to his hotel.

Following a couple of hours of sleep, he loaded his
body with weapons and food, including a powerful
laser that could do permanent damage, and he dressed
like a jewel thief. Nestled inside a hollow leather belt
were three grenades, compliments of Mr. Gadget.
Like a ninja, he covered his face. He needed to let the
household feel like it was a normal night on the ranch
and that they were safe and that he was going to his

meeting in the morning. Penn climbed out his hotel window in the middle of the night and went rooftop to rooftop, jumping into an alley a couple of blocks away. He jacked a car and went out to that house, climbed a wall, and slipped inside a window. It was easy and quiet. The next day, come daylight, there were a couple of dead bodyguards, a deceased, evil sonofabitch with a penchant for torture, and some drugged, large, mixed-breed dogs with big teeth. Penn rifled the house to made it look like there had been a burglary. He took their wallets and jewelry and copied the hard drive and cell phones for Intel for the home office. When the CID and the ISI finally got there, the case was opened and closed, just like that. The site was so clean—messy, but no prints, no witnesses, no anything. Shit, except for three dead bodies, some stolen property, and a couple of stoned dogs eating Ruffles potato chips and kibble, nobody could prove anything. It was almost comical. It certainly was poetic justice, and the few local hip CID/ISI guys knew it.

Except the jihadists and the ones on the take, all the cops were happy he was gone. No one would be getting a kickback. There were a couple of guys in the CID/ISI that were decent human beings and good agents. They knew what was up and were secretly jumping up and down that one more parasite had been removed from their circle. They loved their country and were very upset at having to raise their children in such a place. At every turn, they were doing all they could to bond with the few families who were likeminded, hoping to drive the religious whack jobs the hell out of Pakistan. To them, what the authorities discovered at the house amounted to beautiful, swift justice, which they secretly backed. Shaking their heads, they pretended to be baffled. All the while, they knew whose calling card was left, and they rubberstamped it.

The American embassy got a call the next morning to inform them about some murders that occurred the previous night. Of course, they had to keep the proper authorities in the loop. No one in any of the American intelligence agencies knew anything about it. The ambassador was also notified that there were several bags of Ruffles potato chips annihilated around the dwelling. There were also some very stoned canines on something akin to low-dose elephant tranquilizers that came out of India, making the canines unable to identify any of the perpetrators. As a result, the local police were closing the case. The authorities didn't have a lot to go on. Too bad. Penn was there to find out how far out their web extended. Pakistan, Afghanistan, where else? Who was responsible for all the terrorism?

Days after Penn had been in Turkey on a one-day run, a government installation was bombed by terrorists. It was twenty-four hours following his departure. They apparently had bad Intel, because they missed.

Penn was very lucky. He had always been lucky.
He knew he was always in their crosshairs when he
was in the region. He thought, *wow, I was just there
yesterday, and three days before that.* In and out like
a drive—through, they apparently didn't have enough
time for setup. There were meetings he flew in to
attend. All of the players were so proud of all the new
"toys" developed to help defend the home team. They
wanted to show off more than anything, certain that
such a display would leak back to all involved parties,
therefore making the world a safer place. The world
is safer when adversaries know that the other side is
serious about defending its turf. Deterrence usually is
maintained, and countries know that no one can take
anyone else's shit. Most countries outside the United
States have gotten this message, so they have stacked
their defenses accordingly. When a third-world country
acquires a weapon of mass destruction, the first
thing they do is brag about it, set a press conference,
grant high-level interviews, and make journalists do
cartwheels. They manipulate the worldwide press into
a frenzy.

They like to show off the latest Russian jet that they
bought, invite a group of journalists to tour a military
installation, and parade their soldiers and weaponry
on the world stage. They then expect reputable
journalists to write riveting stories about it all, stick a
flag in it, and call it done. You do it because you have

to, because that is what you're there to get done. And it fosters the relationships that allow you to dispose of some scumbag that truly deserved it.

That is the real mission, and accomplishing it sometimes requires a speedy exit, before people catch on to what really happened. Sometimes they're okay with it, realizing the world is a safer place to be. Sometimes they're pissed, and this is when things get dicey. They feel like they have been duped.

Chapter Eleven

When some asshole gets checkmate, and innocent people suffer, that constitutes a loss for everyone. However, if some jihadist makes an unscheduled exit, and it saves millions of lives down the line, people need to be okay with it. People need to grow up and get real. Penn knew all of this and lived it every day. Through airports and cab rides and donkey rides and trekking in the desert. On private planes and trains and helicopter rides, sexy cars and fighter jets, motorcycles, piece-of-shit cars and trucks and ships, and every other form of transportation you can imagine. Penn did it all regularly. Whatever the job required, whatever it took.

Penn hit the airport coming back from the daytrip to Istanbul. Everything had been going well. He had just over one day left and was anxious to get finished with his last few charges in Pakistan and then get the hell out. It could not happen soon enough, as far as he was concerned. Tomorrow was the best-case scenario, or the next day at the latest. Penn got an escort from the airport back to his hotel and munched on the snacks in his briefcase while sitting in the back of the car.

For once, he didn't even care about food. He just
wanted to get back to the hotel, call the home office,
and describe what had happened earlier. He also
needed to transmit information back to the home office
and was wondering when this would be possible. He
needed to call Aria and lie to her, not telling her that
he had been somewhere else for the day. He wondered
what she would think about his insane running
around and his crazy life, and what it would be like
to have what everyone else pretty much considered
a normal day. He wondered, too, whether she had
normal days like he thought she did. It had been so
long since Penn had one, and it dawned on him that
he really didn't know how to define it. But he had to
admit that just the concept alone was quite alluring.
The sexiness of normalcy—or of what he thought it
was. To be able to wake up and know where you were,
not to struggle to remember what country you were in,
not to have to sleep with a weapon—all the little things
that people tend to take for granted. The trappings of
normalcy, the voice of a day.

What Penn did not know yet was that Aria was not
what most people would consider normal, not by a
long shot. And it was a good thing, because what Penn
wanted had nothing to do with normal anyway; he only
thought it did. In fact, as defined by most people, it
had absolutely no place in either one of their worlds.
Most people think they would sign on for a wildly

exciting career in espionage around the globe, but in reality, most people are seriously risk-adverse and run from discomfort. It's self-preservation and human nature. Penn and Aria's work required that they run toward danger, that they repel down the precipice, that they walk the line without a net, nearly every day. There were two little rules that both had been taught and both lived by but never discussed: don't look down, and don't get caught. Very simple words, those two rules defined their worlds.

Back at the hotel after the side trip and another shitty Pakistani cab ride from the airport, Penn could breathe, at least for a spell. For all his rough inner dialogue, compared to his environment, he was genteel. Penn was raised in the South. His father was a first-generation European immigrant, and his mother was a gentle Southern lady. He was a gentleman, and his speech, mannerisms, education, and intelligence reflected as much. He could respond like any number of his fellow operatives when the shit hit the fan and did not mince words; clearly, he was no candy ass. He was a formidable intellectual in a Terminator's body with a velvet-gloved gentlemen's hand. This never went to waste back at the home office; he was used as the ultimate spokesman regularly, and he had finally become okay with his charge. After years in the game, he was supremely confident and knew his capabilities.

Penn felt he could handle almost any situation, except navigate with this girl. He knew she was his true north and told her so relatively early. He felt quite literally that he had just lived his life up to now waiting for her to be born and grow into something he could wrap his head and body around. He had to focus a bit longer, and then he could leave. It was all he wanted—to go home safely and to get to her as quickly as possible.

Ahead of him was one more meeting, maybe two, in a hotel this afternoon. Everyone at home base was tuned in and knew it had been set. So much of his job was just that, hurry up and wait. It was usually in God-awful places on the planet. Waiting. Waiting for other people to get their shit together, and then suddenly, *bang,* all hell breaks loose, and you'd better keep your eye on the ball, or you could wind up dead.

Penn got a call from the home office and his chief operations coordinator, Marshal Tedowski, who was blowing off a steady stream of new information and Intel in his ear. Marshal, who was the personification of a shit storm, was intolerant of anyone who didn't have the intellectual capacity or the emotional tenacity to keep up with him. Marshal, who had known Penn for more than twenty years, thought of him as a brother. Like so many of the guys, Marshal was the physical antithesis of Penn. He was round and was a poster child for lousy eating habits and lack of sleep.

He was frenetic in absolutely everything in which he participated. In Washington, a city that pretends it's still a genteel Southern town, Marshal was a social pariah, although he never thought of himself that way.

Washington is a town of professional liars, bullshit artists, international thieves, and whores; it's no place for an honest man or woman or their children. When one shows up at the arrival gate at Reagan or Dulles, alarms go off all over Capitol Hill and Pennsylvania Avenue. An honest, hard-working person who has power and position and is fearless makes everyone look bad. The prevailing attitude is that the person must be crushed quickly, instead of understood. He or she is the proverbial square peg in a round hole. That was Marshal. The issue with Marshal was that he always ran contrary to the program, but he was never a prick. Many people with his job description serve the purpose better if they have the ability to be a sonofabitch. He could play that role but only because he loved his country. He simply expected people to do what they said they were going to do. When they didn't, he would call them on it. This was always great at cocktail parties—and nothing short of earthshattering around the conference tables that don't really exist in Washington. Marshal and Penn were like Jimmy Stewart in *Mr. Smith goes to Washington,* and it wasn't an act. That irritated people. They knew they would never be as good or as smart or as successful. Marshal and Penn were highly effective, with their hearts in it for the right reason. They never wrapped themselves in the flag as a political ploy, as was the current fashion; they wrapped themselves in the flag because they believed in the people and the documents that built it. Penn dialed on his com device, and Marshal was immediately on the line.

"What are you doing, Penn?"

"What are you doing, Mom?" asked Penn.

"What are you, Twitter Langley?"

"I just got back in the room, and everything's fine. Pakistan is still a shithole, no changes to report. Sorry to be the bearer of bad news."

"How did everything go in Istanbul ? What presents do you have for me?"

"I have things from the other night here with our friend who forced my hand, and then I have more from today as well. All the puzzle pieces fit."

"Good. For that, you get a gold star and an aatta boy. You're having a good day."

"How the hell am I going to get this stuff to you sooner rather than later? I'm feeling anxious. I don't want to sit on it any longer than I have to. I'm running out of places to hide shit. This place is a buffet of Intel. All you can eat, and I'm done."

"Nah, make it work. You're outta there within twenty-four. Hold onto it and transmit the rest. Just fly low with the hand-carry, okay? Get it worked out."

"Yeah, fine, I'll get rid of almost everything after. Just confirm transmission for me. I don't need to sweat that too."

"How long before that series of meetings today?"

"Three hours. Shouldn't take very long. The first two should go quick. Really basic stuff. Same place. The third is the change-up. The guy that was fixed by the shepherd. Change of venue, sandy pasture, which way is the beach?"

"Only you would get in so deep within a few days that we're actually dealing with a fucking shepherd. Remind me to make a tasteless joke about this later, something to do with wellies. Affectionately known as sheep fuckers."

"No problem, I won't let you forget. But I know this is one you guys will never let me live down. With my luck, he's an informant who's also a frickin' shepherd, only in the Middle East."

"Just remember, what happens in Pakistan stays in Pakistan. Call me after."

"Wouldn't miss it for the world, my friend. I'll check in after each meeting, and then after the last one, I'll call to make sure that we're still on target for my departure."

"Just watch your ass. Don't assume that these guys are as benign and unprepared as they've been in the past. You can never tell how fast or slow they're going to get with the program. Don't take any unnecessary chances."

"Roger that. We'll talk in a few hours, Chief. Keep an eye on me. I'm a steak guy, not a lamb guy. I don't feel like having any of my last meals be anything but surf and turf. Remember that. Get me the flock outta there."

"You're funny."

"Yeah, it's one of my hidden and more endearing qualities. Don't tell anyone. Talk to you later. Roger that, I'm out."

Alone in his hotel room, Penn proceeded to put things in order as he would need them, laying them all over the bed. Notebooks, his laptop, pens, files to review before each meeting. He hated being unprepared, so he routinely over-prepared and sweated it terribly when he did not have proper time to prep. It never mattered what it was he had to prep, he would freak out. He laid out his clothes for the three interviews. He would be playing the part of the bumbling, inquisitive journalist. For this gig, however, he would be wearing his token garb to complete the picture for them. Turns out that this would be a good thing, because part of his uniform journalist gear, even though it was summer, was Kevlar.

Though it's light and thin for what it is, it's still a bulletproof vest, and it's bulky and hard to disguise. It was always a challenge to keep it under wraps. A vest was hot and a total pain in the ass to wear, but Penn was happy to have the option, and he was smart enough to know that he should use it whenever he was in the Sandbox. So he did.

Days enumerated with meetings like today were always a crapshoot, so it was better to err on the side of caution. He never told Aria anything. He certainly did not tell her that it was busy today, and that he was digging in for the last twenty-four hours and talking to some really creepy guys to get some more Intel before leaving the country. He never said a word. He talked about the weather or sex or what she was doing. Never, ever about his movements or what he was responsible for or thinking about doing. Penn never told her where or when he was going or when he was coming home. He never told her where he was flying into. If he did tell her anything, for operational safety, he would lie. Total bullshit, she got used to it. After a while, he figured out that she knew he was basically full of it. For his job, he had to be. When he figured out that she had already surmised all this, he stopped bullshitting her, just like that. From somewhere in Europe during a trip later in the year, he made the jump. He just didn't say anything. She would respectfully ask him questions, and he would answer what he could. What he couldn't, he figured out that she already knew the answers to anyway, so why bother.

Aria woke up sick on this day. Thinking about Penn and waiting for him to call her all night long for the past two days had been catastrophic. She was hanging over the toilet, begging the powers that be to make her vomit. She was cabled to the bathroom as if Mexico had been a recent vacation stop. Her stomach was completely out of whack. She was having frightening, violent nightmares. She was pale white and looked like a vampire. Her mother saw her and how gaunt she was and suggested maybe she see a doctor. Aria got upset and said she was fine. Aria knew that what was happening to her was based entirely on Penn, the man whom she had just met. Her body was flying red flags. She was worried for him, because she understood in advance exactly what was going to happen to him, and his very survival was going to be on the line. This was not an acceptable situation from any point of view.

Aria was debating when and how to tell Penn, and if she should even say anything at all. If she did, everyone would hear her. Home office was always on the line. They would think she was a spy, not a patriot. She would scare the shit out of everyone, especially Penn. Since it was his ass that was actually the one in the field, Aria felt it was important that he not get freaked out any more than he already was. What was she supposed to do? Say, "Hi, I really like you, and I know you don't really know me yet, but I'm in love with you, and you're my soul mate. I know everyone is listening, but you're in mortal danger, and I can tell you exactly what's going to happen to you. I'm trying to save your life. Don't ask me how I know this, and by the way it's going to get really get bad there, so please pay attention, because I want you to come home to me."

Yeah, that would go over really well. Penn was pretty wigged out with what was going on already. It wasn't good, and it wasn't going to get any easier. Aria knew it was going to get a whole lot harder, in fact. He was going to get very uncomfortable with Aria's abilities. It would take him many months to wrap his head around that part of their relationship and fully digest it. Eventually, he would get with the program, and she wouldn't frighten him so much anymore. What no one knew is that she already had predicted many things their first year—including high-profile murders and pregnancies and health issues and all sorts of things the world over. She was way ahead of the curve in many areas and rarely incorrect. It was frightening to always be way ahead of the curve. She was taught to hide her abilities and not to discuss them with anyone. Her mother knew the outcome would not be positive. From the time Aria was a child, she was "just tuned in to the world," as her mother used to say. As a child, she developed a habit of asking a lot of questions. She did it for one reason; she wanted to know people's opinions of her answers.

Two months earlier, Aria had been standing in line at a posh hotel waiting to check in, and speaking with her lawyer before their second meeting of the day. The lawyer had introduced her to Penn during their first meeting earlier that day. Penn was home from his office by the time Aria and her lawyer were gearing up for their next meeting, and Penn was distressed because the lawyer had whisked Aria away. Penn didn't know when or how he was going to see her again.

Penn just knew that he had to find a way to see her again, and as quickly as possible. Aria received a phone call while standing there speaking to her lawyer, which confirmed her prediction of six months earlier. Her former business partner called Aria in a panic. There had just been a murder, and Aria had told him months before in great detail that it would happen and that there would be a violent shooting and more. He hadn't believed Aria. Now he called Aria immediately. The only other witness to Aria shooting her mouth off about it was her lawyer, who was standing next to her.

Aria almost never made predictions aloud in front of anyone. The one time she did, her lawyer was there, and so was her former business partner. The lawyer freaked out when he realized what had just happened, as if she was the bearded girl freak at the side show. He went around the hotel telling her friends and business associates and several high-level hotel officers that happened to be in the group before a dinner meeting. She wanted to be sick. She was embarrassed, but they thought the lawyer was nuts. No one was privy to the whole situation or the warnings she issued to specific people, but the lawyer was. If Penn had known all of this, he would have been stupefied. He thought she was a beautiful creature, and he wanted to sleep with her already. He just didn't think she would ever sleep with him, much less like or love him. If he found out she was a freak that could read the world's collective mind, and his to boot, he would have lost it. Penn was used to a whole different type of danger. Physical danger, he knew what to do with; in fact, he was good at it. But emotional danger was a whole different ballgame. Talk about letting his balls swing. This would not be an acceptable or pretty scenario.

Aria was different. Everyone said she looked like a classic Hollywood movie star and could stand in front of a room full of lawyers and businessmen. What Penn didn't know was that he and Aria were very much alike. She could do it, just like him; she could do it all. She only pretended she couldn't because the world can't handle it from a good looking, straight, young female. Not without using "bitch" as the catch-all, and she was no bitch. She tried to figure out why being competent and hardworking and giving a damn made her a so-called bitch. She had met many women who could be described as such, and she knew she was nothing like those selfish, insecure, and egocentric girls. She always made a choice to be kind. One of her favorite quotes was "Kindness should never be mistaken for weakness." She always thought her qualities made her different and desirable. But mostly it just made her vilified by both men and women. If she had been taught to need people more, it would have made her lonely. But in Aria's case, it just made her strong and self-reliant. Aria was a very emotional creature. She was intensely passionate, but never on matters that she deemed unimportant or unworthy. She deemed Penn completely worthy from their very first encounter, and she saw few people as worthy. She understood Penn the minute she laid eyes on him, and there was no going back. It was not even about sex; it was all about character, intelligence, kindness, and the capacity to love.

She knew immediately that if Penn let himself focus, he could love her in the way she needed to be loved. She wanted him to be with her from the word go. Aria wanted to make a life and babies with him from the very first instant. She felt safe with him. She put her guard down and unlocked the door and invited him into her room. Penn had told Aria many times how he played that first meeting over and over in his head, as if on a loop tape. It was one of his most precious memories of them together, and it had gotten him through many days and nights in the field in all sorts of hellish conditions. He would reflect on what he had to live for and why he was alive in this age in the first place. He felt he was alive to finally meet and be with her.

Penn had finished pulling his gear together, and it was time to put together his clothing in order to complete the illusion for the day of the dedicated journalist. On this day, he would don a Kevlar vest underneath and an olive green V-neck T-shirt to reduce chaffing and wick his sweat away, and because it would help spray should he happen to get shot. Then another white T-shirt, and then his collared work shirt and jacket. The whole ensemble was big enough that no one would know what he had on underneath. He took his trinkets that he used for luck and put them in the pockets of his khakis.

He stuffed some food and water in his briefcase. He needed regular sustenance, so it pays to be self-sufficient, especially in the third world. Last but not least, he laid out his weapons, pulling them out of the hidden false bottom in the case he was carrying. He had to speed up now, as it was getting late. He had spent close to an hour testing weapons and organizing his gear, putting on his game face, and running the operational stratagem in his head one last time.

Penn had changed his service weapon before this rotation of the operation. He had been anxious about it until a couple days earlier when he got the chance to test it. He had been in the field in Europe a month before, and he had experienced a problem; his weapon jammed, and the timing really sucked. He looked to the logistics and support team at Langley to make sure that they never ended up in a position like that ever again. So now he was armed with a new service weapon and a 9 mm backup piece. Penn had other options, of course, since Intel operatives facing would-be assassins never like to be caught with their pants down, so to speak. But sometimes it's unavoidable, and then having great hands and feet and a fast head are all that stand between you and St. Peter. He thanked God every day in his own non-religious way for giving him raw power in that arena, and the ability to bring all of it to bear against his enemies regularly.

He thought of himself as a modern-day gladiator. He felt comfortable in the role his whole life, and by now he didn't remember being anything different. His role as a globe-trotting journalist was just an act. That was the part he never felt comfortable in. Yet he knew that his discomfort playing that part probably made him more effective and convincing in the field, because it gave him access to people and places that otherwise would have set off alarms. With his reluctance to display attention-getting machismo, he was better able to blend in foreign capitals, especially in that part of the world. He had absolutely nothing to prove. He was the alpha male in every room. Unless God decided to pop by. He never needed to prove it. He spent his time trying to confuse the bad guys and show them why they were the alpha males under their flowing robes. He knew better than to beat his chest and just eat their heads; it would have been just a little too Captain Obvious, and he would have gotten substantially less Intel to turn in. It would all be wasted on those guys anyway, as most of them were mouth breathers. They thought they had much more intellectual capacity than they actually did, because of the amount of hangers-on that most possessed. The oil money that even mid-level sheiks and their henchmen controlled in the Middle East was formidable. There was no shortage of people waiting around to tell these men how fabulous they were and to meet their every need and stroke their egos.

One last check of his on-person weapons, and he closed his multi-pocketed leather case. He then zipped it closed and grabbed his key and moved toward the door. It was game on. Passing through the lobby, he tried to blend in. Penn hopped into a cab and headed toward the first of two hotels, the agreed-on location for the first two meetings. The place was about ten minutes away, but in Karachi traffic, it could take an hour. He needed to be on time like a regular Westerner, because that is what they would expect, but he shouldn't be early. That would be a grievous error.

Not helping the bad guys to make things easy was always key. Don't make it easy; make it hard. That was his mantra. The trip over to this particular hotel always fascinated him—the shiny, dilapidated buses of silver, the shabbiness of everything, the extreme poverty. He could never get past it. It sure didn't look like Orlando or Vegas or any other city in the States, where an entire prosperous way of life had grown up around one singular act and business. He lamented that in this part of the world, the ruling class had never been one to share its wealth with its citizens. Strange, because the amount of oil money that flowed was immense.

Here it was all about greed and collusion among hypocritical religious zealots. As Penn stared out the side window of the car transporting him, he imagined the whole otherworldly spectacle as a colony of filthy cockroaches—only the roaches were people. The reality of the situation was even worse. The top echelon kept everything and starved the rest. If you tried to move within your social group, you were systematically slaughtered. A little different than Orlando and some guy who drew cartoons, bought some swamp land for pennies on the dollar, and made kids happy on roller coasters. The contrast was staggering, and it continually blew his mind.

The cab stopped in front of the first hotel. There would be one more meeting after these two, and then tomorrow would be here, and he could go back to the airport and get the hell out. He couldn't wait. He entered the lobby and headed for the restaurant. They were waiting for him, and after some brief introductions, he interviewed his "sources" for the magazine article that they believed he was developing. All went well, and no suspicions were aroused. It was a quick turnover, and both meetings went off without a hitch. It was a relief, and after a while, Penn packed up his stuff and made his way out of the hotel. It was getting late in the day, and he needed to change locations. He hopped into cab number two for the day and took the short trip across town. Penn shot Marshal a text message on the way to let him know what was up and that he was on target for the day.

The cab stopped in front of Penn's destination, and out he popped. Upon entering the lobby, he assessed the situation. No signs of trouble, and it was as comfortable as anyone could be in an operational situation in Pakistan.

Meanwhile, back in the United States, Aria was standing in the kitchen with her mother when she suddenly breathed in deep, turned white, and grabbed for the sink so she didn't fall over or pass out.

At that same moment, half a world away, back in Karachi, Penn did the same drill again, slipping into a bathroom to empty his bladder before anyone became aware of his presence. Then he headed up to a room that was reserved for a press event. He arrived at the room without incident and on time, went in, and met everyone. He greeted everyone, and before you could say, "Karachi sucks," the energy in the room shifted. A bearded Arabic-speaking waiter of Middle Eastern origin showed up with a towel on his arm, under the guise of bringing them something to drink. He approached Penn and at point-blank range shot him in the chest. First, his would-be assassin pulled the trigger, and time stood still. In that instant, three things flashed through Penn's mind: an intense longing for Aria, how proud he was of his two daughters, and how the force of the large caliber bullets knocked him onto his back. Penn's mind was fully engaged, in the moment that seemed like it took a hundred years, when you realize that you're going to get shot, when you're pissed off and adrenalized. Then you get shot, and you know things are immensely fucked up. If you're not dead yet, you realize you're shot, and you try to figure out if you're either dead, dying, or going to die.

Once you establish these watermarks, you react accordingly. Penn had spent his entire career preparing for this moment. He was all by himself, alone in fucking Karachi. It couldn't be a hell of a lot worse—unless he had been targeted for torture, followed by a televised beheading in some dank, stinking Al Qaeda stronghold. They came after him; the hit was that specific. Little did they realize, they were in real trouble now, because he was alive, he wanted retribution, and he wouldn't stop until he got it. Laying on the floor, it dawned on him that he had just survived a point-blank scheduled hit to the chest, and he was alone in the room, and somehow by the grace of God and Kevlar was alive. He hurt like hell, he was out of it, he had bruised ribs, and the wind was gone from his lungs. His head was spinning, but fuck, he was alive, and his triggerman thought he was dead. Really dead, Elvis dead. Now the triggerman was in really deep shit. After only a few seconds, Penn exploded from the floor like a rocket booster.

He hauled his huge body up and made a hasty getaway in the most serious act of self-preservation he had ever faced. He had to summon the cavalry to come get him the fuck out of Pakistan. If one executioner knew who he was, there were others who did as well. Out onto the street and down a back alley . . . where the fuck was the car? He yelled at Marshall in hushed tones. He needed out immediately! Never fucking mind whatever else was on the agenda—they were just shooting at him. It seemed like hours before the car showed up. Finally, Penn managed to get back to the hotel, assisted by two heavily armed bodyguards.

He dumped his gear on the bed. He wiggled himself out of his vest and shirts and climbed into a hot shower with friendlies posted nearby. There could be no screw ups from this point, or he would be toast. It would be a matter of distracting himself in the hotel room this night so he could get the hell out before the crack of dawn. It was the longest night ever. The plan was to get Penn out of the hotel before dawn, and until then, there wouldn't be whole lot of sleeping going on. Penn's biggest fear was that another jihadist might find out his location, and there would be no getting away again, and everyone knew it. His teammates were ready, and so was he. Until then, he was trapped like a rat in a shitty little hotel room. Penn crawled the walls the entire time. The night could not have seemed longer.

He spent time on the phone, swearing like a sailor in real time with Marshal—what had gone wrong? He decided against taking any kind of painkillers for his ribs, even though sleep was not going to happen this night. He called Aria and lied to her, telling her he was fine, just a little on edge. "Tough day," he said. She knew that he was deep in the throes of lying his ass off to her in the name of operational security. He was blowing protocol by calling her in the first place, but he had just taken a point-blank hit and didn't know if he would survive the night, so he figured that bending the rules a bit and calling her to calm himself down was no big deal.

He told her that he couldn't wait to leave, that he was finished there and quite satisfied with everything he had completed. He felt like he had done his job and that he had been successful. He was tired and ready to come home. He was excited about meeting her in Washington. Aria was consciously making the effort to calm him down and make him laugh, even though he felt like a long-tailed cat in room full of rocking chairs. Throughout their entire conversation, Penn had been alternating between pacing and packing and obsessively repacking. Aria was hyperventilating on the other end of the phone, just like him. She knew he was trapped in that room with an evil world outside, and she was praying for the safety and skill of those charged with watching over him until he was on that plane headed home. She spoke to him such sure-footed fervor and clear head. She knew he needed her, and she never let on about it, not once. She was the one he chose to call when he was at his most vulnerable, not a family member.

They spoke for as long as it was safe to do so, and they hated when they had to hang up because of security. They had to watch the clock. Aria stayed awake all night until she knew he was safely in the air, and then she went to sleep and slept like a newborn. Penn was finally where he needed to be, safe and up in the clouds. En route home, Penn slept a little, but only because there had been no sleep the night before, and he was exhausted. He slept because round one was over, and it was terrorists zero, super heroes and angels one. Marshal was on the tarmac to greet him. His big, round, shiny face was a sight for Penn's sore eyes. When Marshal went to bear hug him, he winced because of his sore ribs. Marshal was the only handler in history that could get away with a bear hug on the tarmac. No one dared give him any shit.

They flew into Washington and met people for a short debrief, and then he was escorted to safe place. The love and respect between the two men was obvious. Marshal's best friend was not only alive and upright, but he was a hero too. This was the kind of real-life story that goes on in the agency in their internal version of a history book. A legend was born to right a wrong, and two best friends did it together. It did not get any better than that.

Chapter Twelve

Penn eventually returned to his daily routine after his stay down in Washington, which was liberating but ultimately exhausting. He had a difficult time getting his head together after time out in the field. Penn's most difficult time was making his "day job" worth doing. He hated feeling like he was having no impact. The worst thing you can do to a super hero is marginalize him. Think about Superman; Kryptonite makes him weak and sad. He doesn't know what to do when he isn't saving the world. He loses his place, his sense of purpose. It was a real problem, post-operational disjointedness. It's not just a readjustment problem or about being an adrenaline junkie, it's a matter of being exhausted and listless. People have issues finding their point of focus post-op. Part of it is being tired in a primal way most people cannot begin to understand. The shrinks at Langley knew all too well what Penn was experiencing. The feelings of guilt when returning to a place of prosperity and peace are very real, and it requires considerable adjustment. That was Penn: lights on and no one home, not unlike the way you feel the day before you get the flu. You're just not right. Your eyes are open, and you're there but not present in the moment.

To add insult to his angst, he missed Aria terribly, and he could not wait to see her. Since he returned, he had been speaking to her at least five times a day, sometimes more. She calmed him down and made him feel normal and loved and wanted, all the things that he had not felt in a long time. The women he slept with were mostly cold and calculating, so very NYC. He slept with many Asians, and there was nothing warm or fuzzy there, no deep warmth, ever. Then he met Aria, and it rocked his world. She was like a Latina without the attitude and the bullshit drama. She took care of him and anyone else who needed it.

She was extraordinarily generous with her heart and kind to people and animals, even when no one was looking. It was a testament to her character and how confident she was in herself. He noticed time and again how she continually put herself out. He was proud of that quality she possessed, but he was also very possessive of his time with her from the very first day that he met her. He wanted to go to lunch on his own with her. In his office on the first day they met, he could have spent all day right there with her. No one else need apply. As the weeks went on and they made multiple dates and plans to get together, first in Washington and then in Miami, they got bold on the phone, and he got more and more emotionally naked. Slowly he began to figure out what was happening to him. He finally admitted to himself that he was falling for this girl, even though he didn't want to. Penn felt that he wasn't ready. All the same, he was insanely curious, and he rushed head-first into a journey of discovery, come what may.

He remembered being in denial only weeks before on July 4th when he was at a beach bonfire and some chick parked herself on a blanket next to him, virtually throwing her legs in the air. He had unknowingly outgrown whores of any kind, and it was right before a field trip. In the past, he would have been all over it, but no more. He was speaking to Aria on the phone at the time, and all he could think about was having her there with him, kissing her in the sand in the dark, lit by the huge bonfire with fireworks in the sky. What a drag, he thought, having to cope with this attention-starved woman who kept trying to get him off the phone with the one girl that he had waited his whole life for. The woman bugging him was a pain in the ass. He wanted her to leave him the hell alone, and she would not let up. He finally had to be a blunt, and he felt okay about it. She got the message and wandered off. He thought she would never leave. Finally, what a relief, he thought. He had enough to think about.

He didn't need women; he needed Aria. Little did he know that Aria needed him and would have done anything in the world to be near him. But they would have to wait. There would be a couple of weeks of prep and then another field trip before they could make it official and meet in Washington. The phone calls at all times of the day and night continued. Penn charged Aria with finding the place to stay, and she found a cozy boutique hotel that she would stay at in DC for the first time.

It was a brand-new hotel that no one even knew about yet. Aria was a hider and favored little, out-of-the-way places, high end and hip, but understated and low on the radar, the polar opposite of Penn. She opened up a new world for him in so many ways. Penn would stay in a corporate hotel. Meanwhile, Aria would find the guy who owned a castle and get him to rent her a wing with one key, hers. She loved her privacy and was much more private than Penn. Aria usually traveled alone for business, and this presented some interesting challenges worldwide that were different than those faced by a guy. She learned to be flexible and to hide wherever she went, hunkered down alone in hotel rooms all over the world, for safety, for peace of mind, and so she could control who had access to her time and who didn't. Reading a book on politics while calling her mother from the Stairmaster—that was Aria. Running around a hotel room in a clay mask

and little else with the curtains drawn and doing her
toes before going to a meeting, cranking music on
her computer—that was more her style. Her musical
tastes were schizophrenic, like here taste in men and
clothes. Aria liked everything to be one of a kind, like
her. Different and risky, she was always polished. She
was the ultimate girl next door, but only if the girl
next door looked like she spent her entire life in *Vogue*
magazine. She was so unlike anyone than Penn had
ever dated before that it was almost comical.

Aria was a true patriot from the time she was little
and always had a strong sense of self. Her mother
would say you could always tell in photographs of
her as a young child that she was comfortable in the
world and in her own skin. Aria had an unbreakable
moral compass and held herself and others to high
standards. This was another set of traits that they had
in common. The formative years were very telling for
Aria. In her first school play, she was cast as Thomas
Jefferson's wife. She was immensely irate that they
would not let her play Jefferson. She complained
bitterly to her parents about what a stupid situation it
was, but she took the part of his wife when there was
no other option. She figured out that if she couldn't be
the guy who was responsible for everyone, she would
then be the girl that had the ability to affect him. That
was in third grade; she already had an opinion and
an attitude. When her family offered her the chance to

control her world by decorating her bedroom, she took the bull by the horns. She made sure her wallpaper was not like all the girly girl bedroom set she had been saddled with, all ruffles and blue. She hated blue and thought it was common, so she picked out a pattern. Red white and blue plaid wallpaper with black stripes. All her favorite colors, and black, her favorite for clothing. Aria's favorite dress as a second-grader was black.

Her walls were covered with four types of pictures: fashion pictures from *Vogue* from the 1930s and on, models, boys, and airplanes—basically everything she loved besides cars. She was a sprinter and a gymnast until her legs grew long and coltish, and then she became a distance runner out of necessity. She was like Amelia Earhart on crack. If Amelia Earhart, Demi Moore as GI Jane, and Lara Croft had a love child, it would have been Aria. There was never any middle ground with Aria; it was all or nothing. It was a quality that Penn adored in her, and he felt much the same. He loved the fact that she never phoned anything in, and he loved her passion for life. He probably never would have fallen in love with her if she would have been wishy-washy about anything, including him. The world was full of those apathetic, uniformed people. Penn saw nothing positive in it, and neither did Aria.

The dog days of summer finally came to Washington, where it's so humid and awful it feels like your breathing through cheesecloth. It went from cold to hot as hell to humid and hot as hell. Not like Baghdad or Kabul hot, but hot nonetheless. Aria didn't mind, as she was used to it. Penn, on the other hand, was immensely bothered by the heat, even though he had lived there for years. Extreme temperatures were not good for him.

The day finally arrived when they would meet as they had arranged in Washington. He would pick her up at the airport, and they would spend the next three days together. She had booked her room in the hotel she had told him about. It's background, she thought, was strange, given its colorful history. She called him and told him about it in advance, in case there was a problem. He didn't think so but thanked her for being so attentive. And so it went, Aria boarded a flight at the crack of dawn, leaving the beach and the heat, heading north. She blasted into the sky in the little aluminum tube that would deposit her into the lap and the arms of an emotional free fall. Penn arrived at the airport more than an hour early, over-prepared and antsy as hell.

No one knew how it was going to go down. What would they say when they initially saw each other again? It would be the first time since they first met months ago. So much had transpired since then. She thought about it as she flew toward their rendezvous. What if they did not get along? What if he didn't like her? What if he didn't think she was smart, or kind, or for real, or beautiful? What if she didn't like him as much as she thought she would? What if they clashed, and the heat over the phone wasn't in the room? After all, they still had to work together! What if it was a disaster?

Penn was just as anxious. How she would look? Would she like his cologne? He was so jacked up to hold her. Would she let him touch her? How far would she let him go? Why was he so flustered? He had never felt like this before. Questioning his game, he barely recognized himself. It had been many years since he had worried about a girl. What made Aria so different? What made her so special? Why was he so bent? Jesus! Aria sat on the plane, her stomach in knots, drinking Diet Coke and feeling guilty for doing so. She was in love with him already. What if he expected to sleep with her?

What if she didn't think she could go through with that much intimacy so soon? What if she didn't like the way he smelled, if his arms didn't feel right? If he didn't really make her feel safe, and he made her feel vulnerable? What if he was still seeing half the female population? Holy crap! Aria wondered what had she gotten herself into. *Shit. This was a nightmare waiting to happen. He's going to want to jump me, and I'm not ready.*

The jet touched down, and Aria plugged into her MP3 player to let the music give her some much-needed courage. Coldplay had become one of her go to's for emotional bravery. Aria was tired. She turned off the music and thanked the pilot and crew as she disembarked from the 737. She took a deep breath when she got to the top of the gangway. She hadn't been in Washington in years, and she was so loaded emotionally and so excited that she thought that she would explode. As a rule, nothing scared her, but she felt like she was walking a tightrope over a gorge. She stopped in the bathroom to urinate and check her face and hair one last time. Then she adjusted her attitude in front of the mirror, grabbed her gear, took a deep breath, and pushed herself into the throngs of people flowing out toward the meeting area.

Suddenly, she saw him. Penn's eyes met Aria's. He was really there. It was magic. Nothing short of fireworks at Disney World. She melted all over the floor, and she wasn't even near him yet. He felt the same. They locked on each other's gaze, and that was that. Her stomach did a flip flop. She let out a squeal and ran to his arms. He wrapped himself around her and rocked her like a child. Aria buried her face in Penn's chest like she had wanted to do in May when they met. She drew a huge breath, and then she started to cry. She was so happy he was alive and that they were in each other's arms. The girl who never wept, cried in the airport in front of God and the world. For once, she felt like she was where she was supposed to be, and "home" was there in the airport, enveloped in huge arms of a man she had met only once.

Chapter Thirteen

They retrieved her luggage, and Penn wouldn't let her carry anything heavy. Customarily, she was stubborn as hell and responsible for her own luggage, but she let him carry it for her. She felt decidedly female, and she liked it. This man was actually strong enough to be her man, just like the Sheryl Crow song.

Penn escorted Aria to his car, hoping that she would love it. The car was her favorite color, silver, and it was fast and classic and sexy, like a Steve McQueen movie. Aria's dad had educated her about Steve McQueen, so she understood the gesture of the sexy classic car. The romance, the spirit. She was so turned on. Penn still did not know how much she loved classic cars. This was no brand-new wind tunnel vehicle; it had style, substance, elegance, and grace like Penn. He deposited her in the shotgun seat, and she put a scarf on her head. They looked like a magazine cover. They belonged together. They blasted down the highway, the real deal and the baby throwback. Thirty minutes later, they pulled into the parking garage downtown. Penn promptly argued with the valets because no one but him was parking his car. Aria went inside and registered and got the room. Penn arrived in the lobby, and they took the elevator up to their floor. They got inside and made chit chat, and Aria tried to defuse the sexual tension while they both unpacked and marveled at the sexiness and comfort of the room.

It was her taste and different for him, but he loved it. Mostly, he was just comfortable as hell with her. He emptied his pockets and plugged in his devices; it was like pulling off body armor. They slowly got rid of all the trappings of daily life, drew the curtains, and locked the door. Slowly the clothes started coming off. The point was to make time stop, to forget that whatever time they had would eventually come to an end. The other goal was to close their outside lives out, to live only in this blissful, frightening, sacred time. Getting naked in the shower was her goal. Flying always made her feel scuzzy. Subjected to the bugs of the masses, she wanted to be clean again. Aria wanted to take Penn with her into the shower while she did it.

He didn't know if they would sleep together, but he ached for her. When Aria looked at Penn and said she felt gross and needed to shower, he immediately pulled off his shirt. She smiled and walked toward him and took his hand. Penn held her, and she told him how tired she was because last night she was just too excited to sleep. She asked him if, after the shower, he would be adverse to laying down for a while before they went to find food and water. Penn was all over it and would have done anything he could to get Aria into bed, even if it might take a little while. He just wanted to see and hold her, close to him and naked; he didn't care where or when.

Penn thought they might have sex, but he knew by the time they got out of the shower that they would be making love when it was game on, not having sex. This revelation was quite shocking to him because it happened immediately. It was already so hot between them that they both were doing their damnedest to slow it down. Both of them were so worried about getting burned. They knew that once they had sex there was no going back. They knew the experience would be so intense that everything would change forever, and they would still have to work together, despite their sexual escapades, and things would get very complicated after that.

The funky Carrera marble bathroom took on a warm sensuality from the steam from the shower. They turned to liquid in each other's arms and had their first deep, long, hot, naked, wet kiss, the kind of kiss that makes a lifetime and sextuplets simultaneously. They were hot and melted, and they just wanted to get clean and get into the crisp white sheets. With 99 percent of their defenses down, they felt better. Penn grabbed a towel, while Aria slipped into the white, plush, Turkish robe and wrapped a towel around her head.

They emerged from the bathroom, and Penn pushed her up against the outside wall and kissed her again. Aria wrapped her lithe body around as much of this huge man as she could fit and kissed him back, alternately hard and soft. It was becoming apparent that they were the kind of couple that other people would loathe in public. It was obvious they blissfully happy and hot for each other. It wasn't just the animal magnetism between them; it was the blossoming of a love affair that transcends time and comprehension. They never should have been together in the first place, but they were. Strong as steel and delicate as paper. Their kiss ended, and Aria took Penn's hand and led him to the bed. She pulled back the duvet, and they snuggled up together. They chatted and tried to calm their nerves, fawning over each other's bodies, every square inch, for several hours. They went slowly, taking in the scents, the textures, constantly touching. She rubbed and kissed and licked, bit and tickled him within an inch of his life. They reveled in it. Both of them finally felt safe in each other's arms, and no one was being hunted by bad guys trying to kill Penn in Pakistan.

Penn and Aria were so relieved and exhausted that they fell asleep first, knowing damn well that they would be making hot monkey love for the rest of their lives. Neither of them wanted to go anywhere else; they had found the only bed that either was interested in being in ever again.

Frankly, as hot as that was, it scared Penn to death, but he knew it was right. It was Mr. & Mrs. Smith on steroids. Aria fell asleep in his arms, with her head on his chest like a baby. She had never allowed anyone that visual, since she was a baby. But this was different, and she slept hard and deep like never before. Penn slept like he had not in years; he usually never relaxed, as it was an occupational hazard. They were so alike, it was amusing to them. Many times, they would just look at each other and roll their eyes and giggle. Together, Penn and Aria were lighter than air, and they buffered and protected each other constantly. They made each other laugh like three-year-olds. Together, they managed to accomplish things that neither one had been able to do individually. None of the other people that had come into their lives previously had been able to put their hearts and minds at peace. That was the way they felt, from that very first afternoon with the curtains drawn, wrapped and cocooned in that secret hotel.

The Company called three times, and she bugged Penn to answer the phone. He didn't want to; he wanted to be left alone. But his superiors knew damn well where he was. Back at home base, he had spoken to Marshal and a few close friends about the mystery girl, and everyone knew he had high hopes. Everyone had figured that the sex would be wicked hot, just from what they knew about the way both of these people interacted already. Everyone was curious about Penn's latest sexual toy. Back at Langley, other spooks that he worked with expected to at least hear about the sexual escapade. But in the coming days, the crew would be seriously disappointed.

Penn found himself wanting to protect her and not wanting to cheapen what they were moving toward by telling everyone what was going on. This was no tart like he was used to; this was his best-case scenario, and he would kill anyone who tried to stand in his way. It was clear to him for the very first time, and he was determined. She was going to belong to him if he had anything to say about it. Penn was used to getting what he wanted the world over, so he never had a question about his abilities.

The next three days went by way too quickly, and they were inseparable. They existed in a drunken-like stupor, an existence that took them from the bed to the bathroom to different ethnic restaurants around the capital. For all practical purposes, the rest of the world didn't even exist; they could have cared less, as they were absorbed in their own reality. For two people keenly aware at all times of what was going on around them, they were way out of their comfort zone on every level. They had never gone so long with news and cell phones turned off or ignored; it was truly remarkable.

On the last morning, Penn bolted out of bed in the pre-dawn hours to listen to his voicemails and to place some calls. He was getting an update about his upcoming field trip. By the time he returned forty-five minutes later, Aria was fully awake. Aria hated being left like that, and she felt raw and vulnerable.

Today they would have to go their separate ways, and she was freaking out about what would happen. They had already agreed last night to get together in Miami in a few weeks, but that was so far away. Penn was already in the middle of a full-scale freak out. He was visibly upset at the idea of leaving Aria. He had been on the phone to associates, and he did not tell her that he had to leave early. He just panicked and didn't know what was happening and broke it to her that he would be leaving in a few hours. He was running. Aria was devastated when he broke the news to her.

How could he just bolt like that after what they had shared over the last three days? They were in such a safe place, and nothing in the world could compare with how they felt since they met. She was perplexed because she knew Penn felt it too; he told her so. The hours flew, and when the time came, she walked him down to the garage and watched him drive away. Her heart sank. She wondered how she could have allowed herself to let someone in so deep, only to have him run away so quickly. Brokenhearted and stuck in DC alone, she would spend the next twenty-four hours contemplating his odd behavior.

He left her a day early, and that was a trick she had never seen before. She went back upstairs and called her mom, who tried to make her feel better. Then she put on different clothes and attempted to run five miles on the treadmill. She pouted the entire time. Aria then walked up the street and got food to take back to the room. She barely ate and almost passed out on the street from being so distraught. She would have given almost anything to be able to fly back home that day to her beach where she belonged instead of having to spend another night alone in their bed. She could smell Penn on everything, and it was breaking her heart again and again.

When Penn called her later, she told him she could not believe what he had done. He told her that while driving, he realized he was afraid and that he had messed up badly, that he knew he had hurt her. He apologized and promised it would never happen again. He also asked if she would agree to see him if he came to see her on the beach. She forgave him and said yes and told him that was dying to see him again. She all but told him that she loved him.

The next day, Aria had to fly home. Penn had to get his butt into the office and pretend that the past three days never happened so he could focus. *Good luck with that, big guy,* he thought to himself.

Chapter Fourteen

They both did what they had to do in order to get through the next few weeks. Penn got updates daily from the home office and took many prep trips. He talked to Aria every day, and now they had something to build on. Although they never made love in DC and had only fooled around, they were bonded.

Penn couldn't wait to get through this next field trip and then fly south to convince Aria that sleeping with him would not be a mistake, that he would not be running away from her again. On this trip, he would meet her family. How weird, he thought. But Aria now wanted to push his face into it big time, and he understood why. So Penn was going to treat it as a learning experience and use it as a chance to glean more personal information about the girl he had fallen in love with.

Recon, that's how he would treat the whole experience. She was at the airport to pick him up in a short, hot dress that looked like Warhol threw up all over it. She smelled like Palm Beach—absolutely perfect for him and certainly different than the girl dressed all in black in Washington who looked like she jumped out of a Japanamation Anime sequence. This girl was many girls all rolled into one. She was her own breed. Unique.

Weeks before, right after leaving Aria, Penn ended up on a transport again, following some bad guys' stints in Israel and Yemen. He wound up flying to Russia, where he was escorted almost everywhere he went. He wasn't under house arrest, but the KGB was there among the people in his fray, and it was virtually impossible to tell who was who. These guys were all old-school goons—badly dressed, full of themselves, smelling of Russian pickles, borscht, whores, cheap cologne, and vodka. It was as if they never got the message that the wall fell. It was totally still game on to them, and their supreme commander liked to kill, hit, and poison people worldwide to get his rocks off. Penn had long thought he had a major Napoleon complex, and now he was positive of it. The man was so short, he was basically a Randy Newman song. He must have always had to pay for sex. Turns out Penn was mostly correct. The fearless leader had often paid in one way or another to make a genetic deposit; he was no stranger to the drill.

Penn was escorted from a perfect little town on the sea by creepy, fat-ass guys who had only a few things on their minds. There was an unwritten list in every KGB guy's mind: one was the Motherland, the second was vodka. The third was where the next piece of ass was coming from, not necessarily in that order.

They took him to many locations around the country to observe the manufacturing of weapons, which he was supposed to be covering. Showing off for the visiting journalist was a treat. Screwing with his head and fucking up his body might be even more fun, including getting him drunk and laid. What they didn't know was that Penn was there to do pre-prescribed things, whether they liked it or not. He was determined to succeed at his mission. He had a specific agenda, and it wasn't the one agreed upon by the Russian weapons manufacturers and Moscow. Penn was supposed to do what the KGB had given the green light for with the companies he was covering, so he could be used for propaganda purposes. He was wined and dined in a government-bugged dacha for six nights, pretending that he actually drank six days' and nights' worth of vodka, just like they did.

This made for a great deal of operational creativity. Penn looked for places to put the vodka. Creative imbibing, napkins, plants, seat cushions, anything. One night, they had a reception and showed off the local custom. It was complete with everything a good spy party should have—food, locals, location, location,

location, KGB, vodka, chicks, government folk, and whores.

All Penn wanted to do was leave this bullshit party and find a safe place back in the little town where he could call Aria. Tuck himself in a doorway, find a back booth in a restaurant that wasn't bugged, or go to a side street. That was all he wanted. But instead, he would have to settle for staying at this party and looking for a place to put this vodka he had pouched in the side of his cheek. He motioned that he was going to the bathroom and spit it into some heavy draperies while on his way. One other night, he spit it onto the floor and stepped in it when the two ghouls he was stuck with were preoccupied with a piece of ass.

In this part of the world of social and business activity, the currency revolved around a piece of ass. Penn was offered girls every night at every event. He knew that these girls who showed up uninvited to his room every night and rapped on the door were maybe his daughter's age, and some were even teenagers. They were all potential assassins. Most were victims from the Russian sex-slave kidnapping trade, taken from all over the world. These girls, if they did not die in the initial onslaught, wished they were dead. They were just regular girls, never to be seen or heard from by their families again. They disappeared behind the iron curtain, the real one, which never fell. Only naive Westerners believed the Cold War was over.

They were drug addicted and HIV positive and there to kill him one way or another. He had been warned by the home office in advance and had no intention of screwing around. Penn had one girl he wanted, and she wasn't in Russia on the Black Sea. She was home in the Caribbean where the water was azure and the dolphins jumped in the sunshine, happy to be alive.

Half a world away, Aria was working, worrying, and pacing, waiting on Penn's next phone call. There were once again some pretty drunk dogs hanging around a really nice dascha in the Russian countryside. Dogs always seemed to be around when Penn was present. Bad guys seemed to always have nasty dogs, not just for security, but also for the look. It was as if there were a bad-guy handbook that you got issued when you became a full-fledged bad guy. Step one: buy a few really scary, big dogs. Step two: make sure you sleep in a really scary-looking, dark place with lots of old, ratty Persian rugs and really expensive-looking shit in it. You must complete step one and two before you're allowed to go on to step three and four. Step three: make people come to you. Step four: make sure you get a really hot girlfriend now that you can afford to buy one. Treat every other female like chattel.

The time in Russia wore on, and it was taxing staying in a situation like that for six whole nights. Constantly being watched was difficult, and after a few days, the spy romance had worn off and things were starting to get sticky. They were starting to suspect things about Penn, and it was getting harder to get the mission done. He was being watched more closely. He had to be calm, cool, and collected every single minute of every day and night. That kind of pressure with no relief is very difficult; that's why they sent him, because he was the best. Solid under pressure. Langley knew his success rates, and that being said, they knew that they could count on Penn in a world where you can't count on anything. But even great spies get into unavoidability tight and supremely dangerous situations. It's part of the job at a certain level, and Penn had become a permanent resident.

One night, he thought they had made him for sure; he thought they figured out what his mission was, and he could not have that. But he was out there all alone in Russia with no backup. There were just some wild-ass friendly locals who knew the drill and had been friendly for decades. They were in as deep as deep gets.

Deep inside for years, they knew everything about everybody. One night, it got intense, and Penn knew he would not be alive by morning. He pretty much had a handle on the fact that they had made him. Penn had to get away that night and managed to make it up the road to the friendly locals, imbedded agents that had been there forever. Penn and the guys were sitting around after he got there. They were trying to eat and prepping to leave when they got a crazy phone call and a tip from home office. They thought they were safe and a step ahead of the game, but they were anything but. The guy who took the phone call turned sheet white and looked at Penn. He said, "We have to get you out of here now."

Only then did everyone realize that they were in dire straits and that they would be leaving, right this minute. The KGB had made Penn, and they were mad as hell and coming to kill him. They left immediately, and a pilot dressed as a civilian managed to get his very experienced tail to an abandoned airstrip with an F16, and they threw Penn into the back. The pilot flew by braille, lightless and low and by moonlight. They picked up some safety escorts somewhere over Eastern Europe, and no one ever knew about it. They flew Penn to a base in Europe where the Langley guys were waiting for him, and only then did they learn that the Russians scrambled some Migs and had every intent of shooting down their F16.

Earlier in the evening, he had no idea that this night would turn out this way. All he could think about was sneaking away to grab some time to talk to Aria. He was in a country that wasn't even on his radar four hours ago, but his butt was in one piece. Hell, he had barely gotten out of Israel, which was safe, and Yemen, which was not, much less Russia. He started freaking out about needing desperately to speak to Aria whenever it was safe to do so. Things were on his mind, upcoming field trips from Thanksgiving to New Years. These were going to make Israel, Yemen, and Russia look like kindergarten banter.

He was going to have to answer some of Aria's questions, which he knew would be coming his way. He had many things he wanted to tell her, but because it was still so new, there were only a few things he could share with her. Most things he could never tell her. Of course, she knew this already. But he felt for some reason that she had a handle on him much better than he had a handle on her. Part of the reason for this trip was to test the theory. What did she really know about him? Did she know what he did? How could she when he had never told her anything? He was not allowed to, ever. But she seemed to know almost everything. If she understood, would she still love him? How could she know? Would she still lay in his arms and make love with him when it dawned on her what those hands had also been responsible for? It scared him to death. The thought that she may not be able to deal with it. He knew that he would have to deal with it at some point. He did not want to fall for her and then find out that she couldn't hack the ride. He loved her so, but her leaving and then knowing she existed in the world would kill him. Seemingly no one else in many lands could kill him, and many had tried.

They were going to have to do some serious talking this week, as well as make love for the first time. No pressure, no pressure at all. Once they were finally together again, the days went off without too much of a hitch, although there were bits of drama. At one point, Penn had to go marching out front to the desk because some ridiculous cocktail waitress all but threw a drink in Aria's face and hit on Penn in front of her, twice. He was so upset that she kept treating Aria so badly that he asked for another waitress. The woman was just a bitch, and she looked to humiliate Aria and take her man. She didn't count on Aria putting up a fight or a man knowing where he wanted to be and not be. Penn worked to gain Aria's trust, and after a long while, it worked.

Penn met her parents, and that was successful and strange—having to pretend that they didn't just make love for the first time, that they weren't just like a sappy love song or a piece of prose or a Shakespeare play or someone's wet dream, that they were just people who worked together on a project halfway around the world . . . right.

It was amazing that Aria's father never knew. Actually, he probably did know; he was likely in denial because he didn't want to have to deal emotionally with a relationship like that. Aria took Penn everywhere and showed him all that she could in the short period of time they were together. Forcing themselves to get out of bed given the amount of work, play, meetings, and sex that had to be tended to was not easy, but somehow they managed.

She took him to the spot where she had gotten married before and told him that it was the scene of the crime. He laughed, but he really understood for the first time. Things became real, and the terrible position she had been in before became clear to Penn. It effected his perspective, and he became even more protective of her. Somehow, they always managed to make it work, no matter what kind of problem they had to tackle; it was a defining feature of their relationship. Penn and Aria worked hard to remain flexible, because they needed to stay that way for their relationship survive it's inherent obstacles and continue to unfold and grow. It was an uphill battle.

The day came when Aria had to put Penn back on an airplane, and he had to leave that little beach in South Florida and that girl standing on it, again. But this time, the girl knew that the man loved her and that he would try to make it work because he really wanted her. This time, she cried because she was happy, not sad, and there was a date set to rendezvous again in Washington, assuming of course that he survived his next mission to the Sandbox.

Chapter Fifteen

He was headed to Pakistan, again. It was a tall order for him to come back in one piece, but she believed in him and in herself. She knew there was nothing they couldn't do for the good of the country, if they did it together.

In short order, Penn was back on the ground getting entrenched in Washington and making side trips to surrounding areas to prepare for the upcoming mission, as was customary. Sometimes senior handlers came to him to prepare him, and sometimes he had to go to them. Such was the routine in places all over the world. Little postcard-perfect towns and coffee shops and malls teeming with spies in pursuit of viable, actionable intelligence. It all took place while people shopped for underwear at Target and a garden hose at the Home Depot and got a latte in the drive-through at Starbucks and mowed the lawn and shoveled the front walk of snow. People did not recognize that there were spies virtually everywhere.

As Penn grew more comfortable with his and Aria's relationship, he lowered his guard and would pop off about some aspects of his clandestine work while they were strolling or discussing current events; he eventually stopped lying to Aria for security purposes. Each time it happened, Aria was struck by how people generally were so caught up in their day, that most seemed completely unaware of what was actually going on in the world, oblivious to the dangers. It baffled both of them, how people could be so clueless. How could voters in the United States elect politicians who were fixated on little more than perpetrating their own power base and sense of self-importance. Americans were great, kind people. Most were just seriously misdirected and in massive denial, thinking that the world and their government owed them everything. This ubiquitous feeling of entitlement was like a weight on the shoulders of the guys and gals in the field, and it was something that was often discussed, especially in the annual psychological checkups. Between the stress of work and the lack of support at so many levels for a strong intelligence capability, Penn often wondered how true patriots in Washington managed to accomplish anything and enhance the country's security. Often times, life and death loyalty seemed to work only one way. Thankfully, it was not an issue on Penn's team that he ever had to deal with directly.

There had been many successful missions over many years with Marshal's team, with Marshal serving as Penn's principle handler. But then one day, shortly before Penn was scheduled to perform his next mission, Marshal met Penn for lunch in a restaurant with a heavy heart. They almost always met for food; Marshal loved to eat. Marshal never delivered any news, good or bad, by phone. He knew neither of them would consider this good news. In fact Marshal, knew that both of them would be hurt by the nature of their discussion.

Of course, they could handle it. After all, they were spies for fuck sake. But the news that Marshal had to share still sucked even though they were professionals. The message had come down from the clandestine operations directorate: Marshal's operational status was being drastically altered. The change itself was not out of the ordinary; from time to time, the agency teams expanded, and people were moved, based on abilities, the mission, operational security, and so forth. They never liked to let someone get too comfortable, and they discouraged people from getting too close. It was all so counterintuitive. Unlike many soldiers who do a great deal of waiting and may not ever see combat, with spies, it's game on all the time. Marshal tried to couch the jarring news that the agency was breaking up the A Team, but secretly neither one of them really bought it. Penn wondered what the hell would happen now, and before he could ask his best friend, Marshal told him what was up.

Penn was being reassigned for this next operational rotation to Pakistan, to another handler named Clayton Bullock. Marshal had great things to say about Clay, who was the expert on this specific operation. There was absolutely no one else in the agency whose subject-specific knowledge matched Clay's. Clay was as intimately involved as anyone was allowed to get. He knew this shit, and he was legendary. For him, the situation was very personal, and he had some major demons to exercise. He was a freak like Marshal and Penn. Marshal knew all of this, and despite his loss and sadness, if he was being forced hand Penn off, Clay was the only man on the team Marshal would feel comfortable entrusting with his friend's life. Clay was vested in this operation and would do just about anything to ensure its success and make sure that Penn pulled through safely. Marshal liked Clay's operational style. He was basically the home-base version of Penn, not a field guy. He had the respect and admiration of everyone who worked under deep cover. He was at the top of his game, and he was a straight shooter. He loved his wife. He was a decent human being, working in a world that was a pile of shit. He loved humanity, and he saved lives for a living.

Marshal tried to bring all these positive qualities to the table when he spoke to Penn about Clayton. It was not easy. No need to alarm him any more than he already would be. Pre-game changes are nerve-racking, Marshal knew this. It was his job to take care of his guys, all of them. It was just different with Penn; they hung and did business outside of the Company. They were each other's bromance. They had done all the scary, fun, silly, serious stuff all over the world for years together and laughed their asses off the entire time. They were best friends, and they trusted each other with their lives. All this care and respect took Penn back, and he was happy despite the position he was in. It made him happy and grateful to have Marshal's love and devotion. In a place where relationships like that were frowned upon, he had a brother.

Once you are actually in a situation, you had better not be allergic to adrenaline because it's game on 24/7. Marshal, being the passionate creature that he was, was devastated, but he would never say that. Penn knew, and he was just as sad. Penn always knew who was on the other end of the phone and pulling the levers, the triggers, and watching his ass from every possible angle. It was his brother of another mother, Marshal. Marshal was the brother he never had, and what was going down sucked about as badly as a decision could suck.

This next field operation would be the most dangerous he had ever done. For most people, it would be suicide, which was why they were giving it to him. He was, quite literally, the only numbered agent licensed to kill, and quite possibly the only one who could handle it. The level of his operational participation had amped up greatly over the past few months, and the operation's chief started coming to him with assignments they never considered giving to anyone else. He had attained a whole new level of expertise, including his ability to leverage his cover, and it gave him unparalleled access to places and people who never suspected his real mission. Penn's whole career was culminating now.

He told the shrinks he had a new secret weapon, and her name was Aria. It was a new ball game for everyone on the team with him. They could count on him for his cool head under virtually any circumstances. Finally he was able to control his formerly uncontrollable aggressive and testosterone-driven tendencies. A little bit of seasoning had been very good for Penn. And so was Aria. He could hold his shit now, and he had the experience and the raw power and intelligence to back it up. He was a machine. Penn knew the agency was letting their balls swing on this one. A great deal was riding on this mission, so it was a moral imperative that it came off without a hitch, and that it was not a repeat of a similar situation.

Everyone knew this trip back to Pakistan would
make Penn's last trip look like playtime with Barney.
This trip was so personal to so many people and the
culmination of previous field assignments, amassing
all the Intel to get one specific task accomplished.
If this trip was completed successfully, it would
reverberate throughout the agency for eternity as
payback for a heinous act that was committed years
before. Everyone would know about the outcome.

The day came for him to leave for the Sandbox, and
Penn had the pre-games as usual. He had done a
ton of prep with Clayton, and he felt confident in
the new team. They trusted and liked each other. It
got comfortable quickly, partly because of necessity.
Clay realized what a terrible position Penn was in,
with Marshal's exit right before going out, and he was
sensitive to it. Every time a handler changed, it was a
big deal that no one could ignore.

Aria knew what was happening and had a high level of
distress, as she would have to go through it too. She
had to get used to trusting someone else to watch out
for and save her man's tail in the most horrendous of
situations around the globe. Knowing that Penn was
sweating it bothered her. Aria hoped that Clay was
what she thought he was. Aria secretly hoped that
Clay would be so wrapped up in everything, vested in
the situation and in Penn, that he would never drop

the ball, ever. She prayed for Clay daily and forced herself into his head and loved him like she had loved Marshal. It was important; it was Penn's survival. She needed to support Clay, and he needed her support, but he never knew it.

Chapter Sixteen

Penn hit the ground running again in his favorite country in his favorite part of the world, much to his dismay. Penn got through customs, cleared out of the airport, and hopped in a cab and headed for the hotel. He did not trust the cab driver, so he made a quick assessment of everything around him and then took his weapon out in the backseat of the cab and hid it between his legs. From the minute the cab pulled out of the airport, Penn was assaulted by everything Pakistan. The searing heat, the smells, and the sights really bothered him this time. He still had a bad taste in his mouth from months before when an insect tried to end his life. The cab was filthy, and so were the surroundings. The cab belched blue exhaust fumes. The taxi stopped at multiple traffic lights, and there were dirty, broken-down, old cars everywhere Penn looked. Scooters and people filled the streets. It was overwhelming. With every stop that slowed them to a crawl, Penn felt like they had parked, and his anxiety mounted. Penn kept flashing back to a bad experience in Afghanistan and a suicide bomber he had encountered. The cab driver could be sitting on a serious amount of plastic explosives, ready to take himself out with the white American in the backseat. Even more poetic would be stopping in traffic and being surrounded by all these jalopies and scooters as someone walks up to the car intent on another hit on Penn.

He hated feeling this lack of control. Months before, he had been shot in the chest at point-blank range, and some experiences just have to change you. Getting shot in the chest is one of them. He had not realized how shocked he was or that he had not processed the experience completely, until he was back on the ground this day in Pakistan. But he was feeling it now. He rubbed his pistol, trying to comfort himself. Penn knew full well his usual weapon of choice would not save his ass if there were any plastic explosives nearby. He tried to banish such crazy thoughts, but that was the thing—the thoughts weren't crazy because these things really did happen regularly, anywhere in the world there were terrorists, more specifically, Islamic terrorists. Penn thought it must be ridiculous to be part of a fanatical religious community hell bent on death and mayhem. You would think that with all the Muslims on the planet that they would function more like a Japanese society, by putting social pressure on the bad apples and enforcing consequences upon their violent brethren who despoiled everyone else in the faith. Surely they could affix some social consequences for reprehensible behavior to alter such conduct. This premise has successfully worked with different races from across the globe for thousands of years, so why didn't they do it?

Crazy idea, but Penn thought it just might be worth a shot. This trip would be high profile, and it was something the agency was counting on to help keep his butt intact. It was no guarantee, but it might help. The lowlifes might be less apt to try to annihilate someone they felt would be watched, escorted, and valuable to their cause. These groups are nothing if not opportunistic. They are not necessarily good at capitalizing on it, although they had been getting much better at doing so lately. Since 9/11, the groups both named and unnamed had looked toward their CNN moments. They looked for the biggest bang for their terrorist buck. They looked for the journalist that either doesn't get it, hates the West, or is looking to make a name for themselves. Capitalizing on sensational media had become a function of necessity for the bad guys, manipulating the naive West, but some knew better and had finally started responding accordingly. It took too damn long, but the Unites States was finally getting better at fighting their dirty asymmetrical war. They were learning to communicate better from agency to agency, sharing more information and getting to the end game faster.

Penn thought it was always ridiculous. Here they were fighting a war world-wide that no one group could see or was responsible for, entirely financed on both sides by America and the rest of the West, with its need for oil. And now the current administration was standing in the way of all domestic development, choking off the only shots at a healthy, effective path to support national security. By failing to sharply curb it's appetite for crude oil, the West was helping to underwrite the terrorists' monetary stash to commit mass murder worldwide. It was tragic and brutal.

Penn hunkered down at the hotel, unpacked both his bags, and kissed his Kevlar. He called Clayton back at Langley and checked for any last-minute changes. He had to get some more input on his local contacts and get any updates on the threats that he could be facing. He checked in to make sure everything was running according to the operational schedule and let Clay know that he was okay. After a quick shower and a few hours of sleep, he left for his first meeting. It was the last hurrah for hot summer weather in Pakistan, and desert hot is a whole different kind of hot. He would basically be operating solo, but there would be people close by to clean up the messes when he was finished doing what needed to be done. He also had backup to a degree when he needed it, and though they could never be seen together, there would be people around. Everyone had to be very careful though because these were all "in country" people, and they were buried very deep. Their covers, like Penn's, could not afford to be blown.

Penn had met and worked with the station chief, and he was a friend of Clay's, but it bothered Penn that he really didn't know him. He wished he could have been closer with him at the time. But he trusted Clay implicitly, and if Clay said that he was a real guy, that was good enough for him. Penn knew he might have a chance to develop a personal relationship with the station chief later in the year. It seemed as though he was always in the Sandbox in one way or another. Every time he had some time off and ended up in a more civilized place, the agency just kept pulling him back in. The other local field agents were always in serious jeopardy during these kinds of operations, and they did not get to leave the country afterwards as Penn did. It would be important that they stayed safe, and hidden in plain sight. It was a tall order. Their tasks were very difficult, and senior officers were always amazed after they wrapped an operation, especially back at headquarters. There was always that blissed-out crazy high that they got afterwards, that no one else had a hope in hell of understanding. They would hang and drink and eat and talk shit together whenever they could. But they never allowed themselves to get smug, no matter how daring a mission they pulled off. CIA officers working in the clandestine branch, under cover, rarely got a chance to relax, but when it happened, they loved it. There was nothing like sharing that life-on-the-line camaraderie that very few people on the planet understand.

All the meetings went as planned, and Penn followed all the steps he was supposed to track for this operational sequence to be correct. Part of it was the complexity of the mission, and part of it was the emotion of the players and the light that years of new Intel had shed on the situation. The amount of intelligence made this mission unique. Once it was done, it would never have to be revisited. It would bring closure, and everyone was rooting for Penn and Clay and the whole ops team.

Shit, everyone was so jacked among the few that were privy to the pre-op Intel and briefings that if they could have taken out a full-page ad in *Stars and Stripes* and the *Washington Post,* they would have. This time, just knowing the agency was doing the right thing—and settling a score—would have to be enough. They could not afford a pre-op slip up or any misstep that could tip off the bad guys and let them know that the good guys were coming.

There would be two main meetings to facilitate two hits. Two. Penn turned over the number in his head again and again, trying to wrap his mind around it.

The best-case scenario would be eradication of the
rest of the vermin in the world. But heck, everyone
is entitled to their fantasies. Today's job was two; the
others would be taken care of in due course. Penn
wanted to make sure that the others were taken to
completion as well. It bothered him, but he knew that
was not his job or his call. He wished it was. He knew
what everyone wanted to do. He would have been
happy to have his team be the delivery boys on that
one. Everyone was waiting for the day, and when that
day came, it would completely close the book. They
all dreamt about it, especially Clay. This operation
would be the biggest and most important undertaken
by anyone to date, and this would open the flood gates
for the wrap-up with the past. Penn would have loved
to have been a part of the last operation, in order to
make sure everyone had a poker buddy when they got
to hell, but he also knew that it would have to wait.
He got past his daydream only because he needed to
focus on the task at hand. Then his belly and his head
hungered for food and that restaurant he'd been to a
couple of times where they had that great bowtie pasta
in a light cream sauce.

He liked the restaurant because you could sit in what
looked and felt like a giant green house and watch
the summer sun or be safe and warm in the dead of
winter, looking out through the glass. He wanted to
take Aria there. He was sure she would like it. She was

hard to impress, but he knew that she could also be impressed by simple things. Aria liked many things that wouldn't do it for a typical girl.

Aria wondered which other "name" journalists were in the immediate vicinity when Penn was in the country, because she knew there would be enhanced safety if there was a camera crew. Aria knew no one was there at the time, so she was on edge. She spent night after night awake, worrying endlessly. Both of them ended up getting about the same amount of sleep, even though he was the one in the field gathering Intel. They were like a mother and her baby. Aria slept when Penn did, even though they were on opposite sides of the world.

She paced the floor and waited for phone calls and text messages. Adding to her angst were dreams, visions, and tremendous stress coming from his circumstances in real time or ahead of time. This was the pattern hour by hour, while she tried to work, live, and have a normal day. She was affected by the level of danger that Penn was in, his level of discomfort, where he was, what he was doing. It was so taxing emotionally and physically that by the end of the day, all she wanted to do was to curl up in a ball in bed and shut the world out. Aria would fall asleep just enough to dream about Penn and how it felt the last time he was safe in her arms. All she could think about was when they might be together again and the places they had been and made love in, the places they liked, the places that they wanted to go. They had already been in Washington, Orlando, Miami, Los Angeles, Nashville, New York, Chicago, San Francisco, Virginia, Baltimore, and Philadelphia. They met everywhere they possibly could. A couple of trips to Europe, the Far East, and the Middle East had gotten cancelled because of scheduling problems, but they remained on the list. These were only the places where they had stayed and made love; these did not include the places that they had been together. That list was even bigger list, and it was growing every month.

Aria would dream away the danger that she knew Penn was in. She put herself in her happy place and consciously tried to block the input so that she could at least get a little bit of rest. When Penn really needed her, she wanted to be there for him with an extra push. She would not allow herself to let him down. Aria was never entirely comfortable with the abilities she possessed. Over time, however, they were too apparent to deny. Sometimes it would get comical. Family members and Penn would just roll their eyes when unusual things happened in such an obvious way that it embarrassed Aria.

On one of her visits to Washington in a hotel where she and Penn were staying, Aria turned on the television in the sitting room, even though Penn and she were standing in the bedroom and she never touched the television or a remote. He asked her if she was responsible. She stared at her feet, too afraid to tell him. He knew damn well she was responsible. He felt the crack of electricity go through the air. He watched her every second. He watched her shock herself regularly with cell phones, burn up electrical appliances, and break watches. Penn observed Aria dissecting people from the inside out. It used to freak him out until he realized that she would never use her gifts for evil, and that they could be used to create and control positive outcomes. Aria didn't flaunt her abilities, and most people who thought they knew her didn't. She hid it well because she had been taught that it was a survival skill. The only people she protected better than herself were her loved ones. She protected Penn, from that first day in May. By July during that first trip to Pakistan, she was affecting his world daily, and thereafter, whenever he was on a mission.

Chapter Seventeen

By the time Penn was installed in Karachi the second time, Aria was feeling confident in her ability to connect with him. She spent a great deal of energy helping him steer when he needed it the most. Still, it was intense, and Aria, just like Penn, looked forward to when he wasn't in the field, as that was the only time she was able to sleep, see him, and mellow out. When he was safe and with her, she didn't tear up her belly from stress and worry. She then had the luxury of thinking about things other than the degree of craziness triggered by some dictator or sociopath who lived thousands of miles away.

Penn had already spent a great deal of time on the phone with Clay. Penn checked in with his local CIA station chief. He always made it a priority to get an update on the threat environment wherever he went so he knew what he might be facing. He also talked to his local contacts and connected with anyone Clay told him could be useful. Clay was known for his relationships throughout the world, which was part of the reason he was such a great handler. Clay was tight with the station chief in Pakistan, even though

Penn only knew him in passing. Penn had spoken to media people in country before he arrived, because the Company had wanted this to be a high-profile visit. For this reason, he went out of his way to identify himself as a journalist on assignment in Pakistan.

Penn felt uneasy about the whole trip. What bothered him the most wasn't the mission itself but the question of who he could trust. The biggest dangers were the double agents and opportunists that could be flipped for money. And since it was always life and death in one of the third-world shitholes, it didn't take much to alter someone's alliances.

Joint operations were common. The State Department, the White House, and the Pentagon loved them. There had been more in the past few years, and it produced some successes, but the risks were always greater. You could never know who was really on your side, and command, control, and communications were always serious issues. It could get very dangerous very quickly. To help mitigate the risk, Penn's team went to great lengths to identify the bad guys. You never wanted to be caught with your ass hanging out. Penn and his fellow operatives were laser focused. They had drilled for a full-blown mission like this repeatedly. Tunnel vision was a moral imperative in order to get it done correctly and get out alive. But no matter how much they trained and prepared, Penn was always amazed at how different things could be when it came time to execute. There were always some people who knew what he was really there to do, but not many.

As Penn rose through the ranks with higher levels of clearance, his operational teams got smaller, more targeted, and then mostly black. Things went from grey and hazy to so charcoal that you could not see anything at all. Operations of this nature were not typical, and many were not run through normal channels, chiefly for the safety of those involved. These were bought, paid for, and run from a myriad secure and secret underground locations around the United States and overseas. You could do more, and more with less because of the technology. The differences in the technology from even ten or twenty years ago were mind-blowing, and it made all the difference in what a team could handle quickly and with minimal personnel. The fewer people involved, the better. As Penn took on more responsibility over the past few months, he became more concerned with leaks. With Clay, it had become wildly important, and even though Penn had a "den mother" that tracked his location regardless of where he was in the world, the concept of a smaller, more secure team gave him and his fellow operatives engaged in assignments the world over a good feeling. That was a big plus from Clay's point of view.

All the trouble that Clay and some of the other guys had gone to on this one made Penn feel more confident, if that was possible. To feel more confident about what was basically a ballsy second attempt at a now infamous suicide mission in the bowels of Pakistan was priceless. He expected to have almost no time eat on this trip, and practically every minute would be accounted for on the mission. Getting in and out with his head attached to his shoulders would be the trick, not just getting the job done. Serving as live bait and gathering Intel sucked, but somebody had to do it.

Now that Penn was planted in the hotel room and had talked multiple times to Clay, he reached out for his local mole. Penn was after a specific guy, and the operation wouldn't work without his cooperation. After repeated tries, he made contact. Like his predecessor, Penn was the "journalist." This time, however, he was determined to avoid the same fate that had fallen his now deceased colleague. The mole never knew what hit him. He never suspected he was being used. Operational hazard. Whoops. Penn unpacked the rest of his carry-on gear and the suitcases. He was digging for some the food he managed to smuggle into the country. He had pepperoni, crackers and cheese, protein bars, and candy. It wasn't exactly a gourmet meal, but at least it would keep him alive and allow him to avoid any of the local food for the next forty-eight hours.

The execution of every move had to be precise, and there was a very strict ops plan. Screw-ups, no matter how minor, were not an option. During the planning stages of the operation, there had been talk of escaping over the border following the mission, getting smuggled out. But Penn knew enough about such schemes to know that more often than not they ended disastrously. He would have no part of it. It's always much easier to come up with an escape plan when it's not your ass in the line of fire. All the same, they also had an abort plan if the shit hit the fan, but after a certain point, he and his team would be committed, period. If things went very wrong, he would milk the journalist cover to the hilt. Not that the strategy saved his former team member. Penn knew full well that he would be walking a guide wire at altitude with no safety net.

Within a couple of hours of his arrival, Penn made a bee line for the local CIA operating base, first to check in with the station chief so he could get a visual. Penn was cleared and was admitted access. He was buzzed through and came into the lobby, and Chamberlin's first in command was sent down to the lobby to pick him up. Chamberlin's guy was different from the support personnel you usually encounter in the field.

At home, these operatives would be dressed nicely. But in the Middle East, you had to dress comparatively shabby to avoid being an operational hazard. Making yourself or your teammates a target for your vanity was definitely not an option.

Standing out was a problem. Chamberlin Forester was a tall guy, probably an ex-operative and a lifer. He was smart, polished, focused, sensitive, and aware. One of the survivors, he was somewhere around sixty, a friend of Clays, and he knew where every single body was buried. That in itself was amazing because in this part of the world, there were so few people that had any real history, and there were so many bodies buried. Chamberlin was savvy to all the players on every side. This made him valuable. He was also very even keel in an extremely hot-headed part of the world. Penn was aware of this and was happy as hell to have him as an ally. Penn imagined that Chamberlin knew everyone and their mother back at home office, and he probably knew the guys who knew the guys. These guys had been in since they were kids, and every last one of them knew what was going on. They had seen it all, and they were fascinating to speak with. Some of them had actually started out in mailrooms back in the day and had worked under many administrations. They all knew each other, and there were only a handful of them, so they founded what amounted to a private club. Penn hoped for more of a relationship with Chamberlin in the future.

While at Chamberlain's office, Penn had a video conference with Clay and picked up the most current Intel from the Israelis, the French, and MI 5. There were a few addendums but no issues to speak of. Primary targets of opportunity that comprised different parts of the same puzzle, protecting national security, and GWOT (the global war on terrorism), in military parlance. It was always interesting to see who had which pieces, who would share, and the Israelis by nature usually had the most overlapping details with the United States.

Penn got use of an empty conference room for the day, which allowed him to make secure calls to Clay, and some junior assistant to Chamberlin kept Penn in constant supply of food and water. This was the support that Penn always appreciated. The table in front of him was strewn with papers and remnants of all types of food, making it look like a small woodland creature had taken up temporary residence. With all the Intel Penn had to get through, he needed a steady stream of nutrition to counter the extreme jet lag and time difference. He kept forgetting he just got there, today. Eating with one hand and working with the other, he did Massad Intel first, since it tended to be fresher. He figured most of the Intel gathered by

Company case officers back at Langley and anything new would be raised by Clay during one of multiple phone and video conferences.

Both teams were always balls to the wall 24/7, and people died regularly trying to attain the unattainable, because they knew there was always that one piece of Intel that would make a real difference. The average American will never know how many people in different places have sacrificed themselves to help save humanity for another day. The unaware just get the benefit of another smile, another sunrise, another breath.

Most of the rest of the first day for Penn was spent at the office, setting up meetings and following up for the umpteenth time with the contacts, and putting all the pieces in order. What Penn and Clay did was akin to moving chess pieces, and the world was a giant board. The pieces were constantly moving, and they tried their best to think three moves ahead, even though it seemed that the pieces blew around the board with no rhyme or reason in real time. This was no game, and there were no rules, and there was no stopping. The only thing that would stop the "play" was death, which is the debt that Penn was sent there to collect on.

Chapter Eighteen

Aria was doing research in between work and learning things about people and the agencies that a lot of the guys who were in now didn't even know—the history of the clandestine services, the who and where, the remarkable people who had given their lives to the service in defense of the country. It calmed her to know these things and to fill her head with the stability of the past, of the people who had come before them. It revved her engines just to connect with these ghosts, because at least then she could feel that she and Penn were not out there all alone. The lone wolf went looking for her wolf pack. Then she met Penn and everything came together. Aria strapped on a piece and became part of The Wild Bill Wolf Pack. All the way around, it was a match made in heaven. The alone but not quite alone thing seemed to be just what Penn and Aria needed. For the first time in both of their lives, they were definitely not alone. They were together, and they had each other. They understood each other, and thankfully the agency seemed to be enlightened enough after a while that they got it. Their response in the end surprised everyone, including Penn.

Penn had done all he could do at the office for the day, and tomorrow would be the operational day. Today the goal was to find a place to eat and crash so he could be up before the crack of dawn to prep for one hell of a day. He said his good-byes at the station, and as he was making his way across the lobby, he bumped into a friend, another agent that he was stationed with in Europe earlier in his career. Neither one had any idea that the other was in Karachi. At first they barely acknowledged each other to avoid drawing any attention. They made their way back into a safe area of the building and promptly dropped the cover and formality. Penn lit up like a Christmas tree, and so did Mike McCarthy. He was from Boston and spent the beginning of his career training to lose his thick New England accent. Unlike most Massachusetts residents, Mike was a Republican, and he did not miss that about home. He wanted the government the hell out of his personal life, and he never made any bones about telling people where to put it if they tried to control or intrude on his personal space. This straightforward manner and independence is what Penn loved most about Mike. Zero tolerance for bullshit, and he always told the truth. You always knew where you stood when Mike was around. Penn never knew that Marshal had been Mike's handler as well, before the handoff.

When the friends saw each other, it was if they had not spent years apart, in and out of Washington. Not being allowed to keep operational tabs on each other was hard on close friends. Within the Company, things had become so compartmentalized after 9/11, for security purposes, that tracking or finding anyone with whom you were not directly involved with operationally had become a matter of state. It was a total pain in the ass. It impeded everyone's communication. That, coupled with the Internet, took away even more of the personal in-your-face trust that is the backbone of operatives in the field. Often it's a matter of life and death. Everyone had become afraid to speak to anyone else. Though everyone knew this was the way it had to be, no one liked it. All of the agents working in the clandestine division took every opportunity to creatively bitch about it and safely bend the rules when security was not compromised. It was hard because the men and women whose lives took place in the field needed each other, on and off the road. Even though they couldn't share operational details—everything was on a need-to-know basis—theirs was an exclusive brotherhood. There were so few of them, and everyone was almost always far from home. So when you see someone who is safe to speak with, who knows who you really are, and you don't have to pretend, it's comforting. Everyone knows what not to ask, and it's liberating as all get out, almost restorative.

For a short time, you're able to pretend you live a normal existence, because everyone does the same thing for a living. Everyone in your group gets to pretend with you. It's "Let's play normal," and the option is so much fun that when they know they are going to get to do it together and not be lonely for a change, they all get excited, and the group always grows. It's just like when you have an informal dinner at Langley. You're in front of your own kind, and it's safe. If it's not a working dinner where you have to be "on" the whole time, you can relax. It's the next best thing to either your childhood kitchen or to your wife's kitchen.

Penn and Mike arranged a dinner for later in the day at a safe place where they would not arouse suspicion. They decided to take Chamberlin's number-one guy, Frank, with them. Mike had known Frank for years, so he was able to vouch for him with Penn. Frank and Mike would swing by Penn's hotel and pick him up in few hours. Penn insisted that it must be early. He had a big day tomorrow, and he didn't want to be kept out late. He could not afford to screw this up. Not going to happen. Penn headed out from the station by a car that Chamberlin had arranged for him—a safe car—a real coup in this time and place. Penn got to the hotel and managed to get in a couple of quick phone calls and a quick nap.

He was still new to country and running on only a few hours of sleep. He still had his boy's night dinner tonight before he could get back and crash. He was happy that Mike had work to do so he didn't have to feel guilty about getting some sleep. That nap would save his butt tomorrow. Operatives in the field and operatives back at the home office often ran on no sleep. Even guys that were sleepers in their "real lives" got virtually no sleep in the field. It was a given—maybe a few hours in a couple of days and then up all night doing crazy shit. It never changed. That, in fact, was probably the only part of the deal that was constant.

In his real life, Penn was a sleeper, he just did not know it. He could never stay down for long, as he would always wake because of his belly. It woke him way before daybreak, demanding food. Sometimes he would wait, and he tried not to eat too late. He was relentlessly disciplined. Given the choice, he would always choose to go to bed early.

On top of the physical workload, the mental workload was formidable. People constantly came to him for his take on everything, including policy issues, defense, threat assessment, issues about dictators of the week. With no alternative, Penn had finally gotten comfortable with this. Penn had become one of the chosen few who knew most of the facts in a computer-driven world where very few people know anything other than what they can look up on Google.

The other exception to this rule was Aria. She was used to being in the same position as Penn.

Like Penn, she was a fair, stable, heady, even-keel decision maker, and being female and young, she was a very odd duck. But she didn't mind so much once she saw that people did the same thing to Penn and to her father. She just took it as a compliment. Still, it sucked her energy, being the responsible one all the time. She tried to navigate the new waters with grace and aplomb. Aria, like Penn, was often gravely misunderstood, and this caused some grief for her. People who met her when she was getting things done thought she was bossy, a bitch, or just loud. But the people close to her knew none of these claims were anywhere near accurate. She was the polar opposite of all those traits. Aria did not speak to hear herself or from a point of ego. She functioned only to serve a purpose, to complete a task. The girl was completely goal-oriented. She believed in economy in everything—movement, speech, work, pain. Everything except laughter and happiness. In those areas, most would never know she was a glutton. Only the people very close to her would understand that she would be the first one to get naked in the sunshine like a three-year-old and laugh like a hyena behind closed doors. She was a maniac, the boy child in the super chick body, and she loved to get life all over her. Penn often returned to a hotel room after a meeting to find her dancing on the bed to a video like a preteen, or dancing around naked with her Mp3 player shutting the world out. Penn woke from his nap. He took a quick shower, dressed, and went downstairs to meet Mike and Frank. They went to typical high-end Middle Eastern restaurant in Karachi that Frank had cleared with Chamberlin. They walked into the restaurant and were thankful they were not the only Westerners in the room. Otherwise, it would have been too uncomfortable. That was the one good thing about the higher-end restaurants and hotel restaurants in parts of the Middle East. If the group was mixed, then you didn't stick out as being the only ant at the picnic. Thank God for small favors.

The men sat down and enjoyed great local food. All three ate like it was their last meal—hummus and pita, baba ganoush and lamb, and the food just kept coming. It was a euphoric feeling in a place where these three were usually very alone and not feeling so satisfied. Penn turned down his normal glass of red wine because of where they were and because of tomorrow's agenda. It would have been nice to get a little buzz, but it would have been careless and amateurish, and Penn was neither. They tried to be inconspicuous, even quiet, but they were having a fantastic time, and they attracted more than their share of attention. After a short time, it was time to go.

They knew from experience that it was not safe to be any one place too long. This was not Kuwait or Dubai, or even Jordan, so God help you if you let your guard down. The guys left and dropped Penn off. He made his way upstairs, making sure he had no one tailing him. He checked his room before and after he entered. Penn washed up, set up the room for an intrusion, and then slipped into bed. He tried to read a book that someone had given him but fell asleep with the book on his chest after about a page and a half. With all the reading he did for work and the amount of information he processed weekly, it was understandable. He just didn't have it in him to ingest any more material in his spare time, all fifteen minutes of it.

Penn drifted off to sleep with thoughts of going home to his girls—his two daughters and Aria. There in Karachi, he was grateful this first night that he was alive and going to sleep in a bed with a full belly. Not too bad, not too bad at all.

Chapter Nineteen

Morning came too quickly, and he was up early. Penn packed his briefcase and laid out his journalist attire on the bed. He had a couple of contacts reach through to set up two meetings by e-mail, and one followed up with a phone call. As he prepared, someone with whom he had never spoken reached out to him by phone to make sure the meeting was still on. Penn was informed by the voice that he would be getting another phone call this morning to make sure he was available, and yet another caller would tell him where to be and when. Operations like this always put people on edge, especially in this part of the world. But, much of this operation would be carried out at night, which would make it even more creepy.

He wasn't looking forward to it. With all the unpaved roads and the lack of infrastructure, the landscape always looked like it had been bombed. Typical of the third world, roads were generally rotten and dusty at best, if there was even a road at all. In neighborhoods, there were mud-packed walls around homes, much as existed in the Middle Ages. Some of the worst bedlam was around the Pirwadi bus station; it was always a mess, and Penn did his best to stay away from the vicinity at all costs. Just getting around was a task, a security issue, and nothing short of a total pain in the ass. Traveling anywhere took so much time.

Penn made his calls to Mama Bear and put everything on course for the faithful trajectory. He checked on everything at Langley and then sat down to eat. Luckily he was still so full from last night, he only had a meager appetite. He had packed some cheese, pepperoni, and crackers in a small leather duffel bag. His head always rested easier when he had more food rather than less to keep on his person in a foreign country, especially in Pakistan. Now the drill was to wait. Wait, hurry up, and wait. The first phone call came in shortly before 8:30 a.m. The caller was checking to confirm the interview. Langley was on the phone the whole time. Clay had already been up for hours despite the nine-hour time difference. He was waiting like Penn. They had the newest Jihadi bullshit phone number, and the info went straight from Penn's phone, with Clay on the line, and Clay relayed to Penn's housecleaners on the ground.

The first meeting was set for just after breakfast, and then there would be even more waiting. The clean-up team would be busy this evening. They could not clean up and operate too early, or it would be all over town, and Penn would not be able to get back in time. The bad guys would originally try to set the meeting for 10:30 a.m., and Penn would say he was caught in another interview with someone. But everyone knew it was bullshit, because "the subject" would be working for us the whole time. Penn would ask to reschedule the interview to later, but he would not attempt to change the place. There would be fewer people on the street, and it would be easier to move about. Well, the call came, and they bought it. They let Penn move the time, as long as he didn't try to move the place, so they would still retain the control, the home-court advantage.

Penn left the hotel and proceeded to the first interview. The venue was a restaurant. Penn arranged for a private room. That made Penn's job easier since it's harder to kill or threaten someone in public. Penn arrived by cab and was led into the back room in the restaurant where he met a small group of people whom he thankfully had never ever seen before. Considering this was Karachi, that might keep him from being shot again. Good to know, note to self.

The interview commenced, and things went as planned. Penn planted some bugs and managed to confirm the identities of all at the meeting and meet his objectives. To keep his image and cover clean, however, he never completed the termination section of the show. With the targets confirmed and the escape plan set, Penn got out of the meeting safely, though it got a little dicey.

He called in the LFM, better known as Langley's Flying Monkeys, as Aria liked to call them. The LFM let Penn get to a safe place away and across town, and let the bad guys feel safe and secure till the end of their day. Then, as Penn was back at the hotel planning the next interview and laying out the schedule with target number two for the evening, the LFM swooped in and made the small group of jihad crazies meet their beloved Allah—no plastic explosives or virgins included.

Back at Langley, if they didn't have another group to visit that night, they would have thrown a party around the water cooler, but they were still working. They would be working for a while, because they still had men and women on the ground. The only thing that would stop them would be 100 percent occupancy at a domestic US military base with an airplane load of people who would need a great deal of sleep, a bath, and a sit-down meal.

Penn called Clay again. They discussed the upcoming target and the different scenarios for him getting out of Pakistan if things got a little squirrelly. And things got squirrelly a lot. Sometimes it happens, the shit hits the fan, and if it's been planned for, at least you aren't shocked, and you can react and solve a big problem without thinking.

Clay and Penn wrapped up their call, and Penn waited for the next call from another fixer. This time, Penn knew the drill would be different. His fixer was not the person who called him; it was a new person. Penn thought it was the fixer for the fixer. In Pakistan, there was a web of Jihadi bullshit that went with every situation. It took enormous patience to deal with all the crap, knowing you could get into a tight spot at every turn. They were such unbelievable cowards, hiding behind all of their brainwashed religious crap in everything. It was an unwritten cultural rule, like the Nazis in WWII. Most of the populous just condoned it and looked the other way.

Penn standing there in the window, knowing better than to go out on the balcony, watched the sun set to the west. He thought of home and hoped that before he saw the sun again he would be on a jet headed west, headed for home. The phone rang in his hand, startling him momentarily, because for a minute he was lost in the sky. The caller told him to go over to a specific hotel and a specific room.

He packed the last of his gear and within five minutes in the elevator. It looked like it was built in Europe in the 1800s. Penn was sure that somewhere in the basement there was very tired donkey being led around a pole to raise and lower the elevator. He felt guilty every time he used it. He got over the images of the wretched donkey and the spectral sky and emerged from the hotel into the chaos of the street. Thankfully, it was getting late, and people were struggling to get home for the evening, so the streets were easier to navigate. The time could not have been better.

While walking from the hotel to pick up a cab, he got a call from Clay to let him know that the cleanup team had great success and that the first portion of the operation was complete. Penn was relieved to also hear that the guys were already in place at Penn's next destination. The hotel for the meeting was just blocks away. Penn finished the call with Clay before he hopped in the cab. He never liked to be in a closed, unsecured area when receiving or making a call. Penn knew the consequences of being careless. He never liked to take chances. He found a cab he deemed safe and flagged the driver. He spoke some broken Urdu and told him to drive to a specific hotel across town.

It took about ten minutes, even this late in the day, before all of Karachi had re-emerged onto the streets for the evening. Putting on his game head en route, by the time the cab stopped in front of the hotel, he was as ready as ready gets. He made his way in and strode across the lobby and to the elevator. He looked for any security people whom his advance team may not have noticed or that no one may have told him about. He paid attention to the layout and to alternative exits from the building. He got a room number by text as soon as he reached the lobby, so he knew where he was going, and he knew that someone was aware of his arrival. This was meant to be unnerving, and 602 was all it said. Penn had no idea what he would face when he got inside. For all he knew, the door could have been rigged with a plastic explosive.

He got to floor six and was pleased to see that there was no one in the hall and there did not appear to be a surveillance system. Penn knocked on the door while standing off to the side. Someone came to the door to open it. They asked him for ID in perfect English with the queen's accent. Obviously, someone went to school in London and came from money. That was better than most here. These guys were not like most rookies or low-level planners. The target was an accomplished asshole with a track record.

Penn entered the room, and the door closed behind him. Those inside patted him down and took his briefcase for just a moment. When they were satisfied that they knew who they were dealing with, they gave it back. Then they asked him to sit down and take out a pen and paper and take some notes. The three

creepy guys and Penn had a chat. He was introduced
to everyone, and then, when they felt secure, one
left the room to fetch some food. They figured the
journalist was going to be there for a while, so they
had a captive audience to spew some of their rhetoric
on, for the Western journalistic machine. Once it
became two on one, they never knew what hit them.
Penn had dispatched the gentle persons, and the
cleanup team was already moving into place. Some
came through the front door of the hotel, and some
came through the window. Penn slipped out into the
hall and got busted by a guy he had seen on the way
in. Not good, and so the chase ensued. The best option
was to get the hell out, without getting caught. Penn
hauled ass, jumping out a third-story window. He
ran his backside off going top speed down an alley
and jumped under an ice-cream cart in the street. He
wished he had been wearing his running shoes, but
hey, when it's your ass, you make it work. This was
one of those times.

When he reached the alley and turned down a side
street, he encountered an old man who observed his
evasive maneuvers. He could have turned him into the
bad guy chasing him, but he didn't. Penn called Clay
and screamed at him about his cleanup team back at
the hotel and about sending in the cavalry to rescue
his ass ASAP. He actually called Aria from under the
ice-cream cart, once he was sure he was safe. Shortly,

the team showed up to retrieve him. They were both on the phone with Clay and his team, almost the whole time. Penn was then taken to a safe place to wait until his unique and exceedingly private transportation situation could be arranged out of the country. No one on this team under these circumstances could say enough about private aviation. It was a beautiful thing, and Penn was about to experience the most exclusive baggage-recovery service on the planet. There was no going back to the room to retrieve his baggage and personal effects, so someone was sent immediately. They packed his gear, tore the room apart, and got out of there. His bags would then meet him wherever they decided to take or send him. No one knew where the second jumping off point would be yet. If it wasn't someplace in Europe, it would be someplace back on terra firma USA. Everything would be perfect. This was what you called a job perk.

Penn was regularly in a position where he ended up losing things or being re-routed or having no clothes in a foreign land during an operation. So when these little problems reared their nasty heads, things would just show up. Penn would be somewhere, and suddenly he would get a gift bag, just like at a Hollywood Oscar party without the face cream and the expensive shampoo. Here's your custom-sized tux and shoes and all your clothes and toiletries, and they are in a new carryon case. It was definitely one of the better perks of the job, but considering the tradeoffs, which could be bloody, it was really the least the group could do for their top dogs.

Penn waited in the safe place with a small team, and then everything was in online, courtesy of Clay and his team back at the home office. Everyone had been walking on eggshells, and the local team was anxious to deliver Penn to his next group of handlers. It wasn't always so glamorous. In fact, most of the time, it wasn't. It just worked out that sometimes it got crazy hot, very fast, and it worked out with the other big dogs able to get in low under the radar and assist. So many times, Penn had to get his own ass out. In fact, those contingencies were always discussed and planned for, just in case, because you absolutely never knew how it was going to go. It wasn't even possible to tell once you got on the ground. Things were so fluid all the time that you just had to wait and look around and see what was going to happen.

Clay always tried to discuss and plan for as many contingencies as possible. The team waited until late in the evening and then put Penn in a car in a hidden compartment in the back. Clay had told Penn and his locals that it was now time to get out and that there would be a hello waiting for him at certain coordinates, and that it would fly him safely over the border into India, where he would be picked up.

Clay had quickly cleared everything with the Indians and found the chopper and the bilingual pilot capable of flying with no lights in the darkest night. Clay had helped save the day, or at least the second half of it. Clay would monitor the whole operation from the sky, in real time, and know exactly what was happening every minute. The pilot would be foreign, but he would be flying Penn to a safe place. All of Penn's fears were quashed before he got a chance to think. He just wanted to get the hell out. Like Penn, Clay and everyone else on the team was cracker jack. Clay knew he would not breathe until Penn touched down in India. Then it would be a full-team sigh—not relaxation yet, but a sigh.

Once again, they would fly low under the radar, and it would be dicey; Al Qaeda and their sympathizers loved their shoulder-fired rocket launchers. And they had plenty of them and knew how to use them, which was a constant source of angst for all the good guys. Looking for buried weapons was like a daily Easter egg hunt.

The local team got Penn out to the coordinates issued by Clay's office, and that was the flight line, in the middle of nowhere. The trip out, while relatively short, seemed to take forever. No matter how well prepared everyone was, they were extremely anxious under these operational conditions. Nails were often bitten to the quick.

Time went by, and they were driving without lights. Thank God the moon was high that night. They started to get close to the pre-determined coordinates, so they needed to slow down and watch the sky to the east. They pulled off the road and cut the engine when they hit the mark. The agent riding shotgun pulled out tiny night-vision binoculars and scanned the sky to the east and the south. He watched the American-issued, unmarked military chopper fly over the brown, mountainous desert like a shadow in the night, out of nowhere. Like a vampire bat, efficient, aerodynamic, quiet and faster than you would expect. It reminded Penn of the national symbol, even in the dark—a huge eagle, proud and strong, with big wings and ultimate control over itself, not giving a damn, always working to be on the side of right.

Penn was proud to be a part of operations like this, especially when things went so well. Even though Penn's activities were often blacker than black, he liked to be a good guy. Everyone understood that some data points were better left unknown and unsaid. It was a bit naive and insane to think that Americans, everyday people, could process or handle all this violent craziness. Contrary to popular belief, the world is a brutal and nasty place. All the field operatives were trained to deal with and process all the stress. Penn felt good about protecting people, and he always tried to do the moral and correct thing. For the most part, so did everyone else. After what seemed like an eternity, the chopper got close, and the pilot and the ground crew both had visual and acknowledged. Langley patched the pilot through to the guys on the ground, and he hovered before setting down. At the last minute, Penn jumped out of the vehicle and ran for the chopper, with Clay in his and everyone else's ear.

The door to the chopper flew open, and Penn took the shotgun seat. He buckled in, put on his headgear and helmet, and waved to the men that helped save his life. Even if he never saw them again, he would never forget the three or four hours they spent being watching over him. He figured out that one way or another, he would run into these agents again, probably in Pakistan. Penn would have been good if Pakistan got put on his list of no-go places, but he was more experienced than that, and he knew he would be back again. It was just a matter of time.

They lifted off, almost silently, and headed east and a little south. It would be hours before the sun was up. Penn took a moment and looked back at the ground where they had just come from. He watched the guys fade away into a dot in the distance. He thought about standing in the window back at the hotel before. He took his first breath and had a hard time not letting the sound of the rotor and the rocking of the helicopter put him to sleep. Before long, they would cross the border. He felt blessed to be with such a safe and highly capable pilot. The pilot had introduced himself as Rupee, and everyone on the line got a laugh.

Penn would never again have an issue with Clay's ability to run him. He got Penn's vote times ten. So while he was on the line and so was everyone else as they landed in India, Penn thanked Clay and the team, on air. "Gentlemen," said Penn, "I want to take this time to say thank you to everyone on air and everyone who put all of this online. Thank you, Clay." Penn asked for a quiet line, and Clay knew to block the Indian pilot's access to the line momentarily. He said to Clay, "May I go ahead, sir?"

"Penn, you are secure," Clay replied.

"Now how did we do with clean up?"

Clay replied, "Nothing but net, buddy. It is a beautiful day, thanks to you." "Fantastic. That makes me happy. I know this was very important to you and to everyone else, and I'm proud to have been a part of it. Thank you for the opportunity and for believing in me enough to let me try."

"Thank you, Penn. It was everyone's pleasure. You righted a wrong today. You're having a career-defining moment, so enjoy it. You deserve it. Now let me switch on the line again and speak to Rupee. Are we good?"

"Yes, Clay, we're good."

"Hi Rupee, this is Clay at Langley again. You're within range. Are you comfortable landing at set coordinates?"

Rupee replied, "Yes, sir. Roger that, I'm fine with it, and conditions are favorable. Anything that I should know about?"

"No, Rupee, everything's online. Our team will be at set coordinates to pick up Agent Penn. Thank you so much for your service; you really bailed our happy butts out on this one. Please thank the colonel again for me, and regards to your wife. We'll see you in a few weeks. Okay?"

"Okay, thanks, Clay—sir. We will see you soon. Agent Penn, when we get down, I'm going to shut her down. Please wait for the blades to stop before getting out."

"Fine. Thank you, Rupee. It's been a pleasure. Hope we get to fly together again under more optimum circumstances."

"Yes, me too."

The team pulled up in a large, black, bulletproof
Escalade, and a few agents got out to retrieve Penn
from the helicopter. The blades slowed to a stop. Penn
shook Rupee's hand and handed over his headgear
and helmet. He opened the door and waved as he
walked away. He turned toward the Escalade and
finally took a full breath for the first time in thirty-six
hours. He was greeted by all three of the field agents.
The moment he climbed into the backseat, he was
handed protein bars and water by the top dog, who sat
with him while one of the other two agents drove, and
the third rode shotgun.

Penn sank back into his seat and let out another sigh.
The sun was starting to come up, and Penn reached
for his sunglasses. He was not ready to see daylight
yet since he had not slept. He felt like a vampire and
knew that it would be a different world for him after
he managed to get some rest. They were headed for a
secure diplomatic location to allow Penn to shower,
eat, and get a couple hours of sleep, after which
they would put him on a flight to Dulles Airport in
Washington DC. It had been another day, and he was
still here.

He knew Aria had been waiting, so Penn shot her a
text as soon as he got on the ground in India. Now it

was her turn to take a breath, and then another one. Several hours later, Penn boarded an airplane and was never so happy to eat boring commercial airline food. He called Aria the minute he got his seat on the airplane. He told her that he loved her for the very first time. Then the cabin door closed, and he had to hang up. But Aria blurted out the perfect reply, which made him a sleepy, happy man. There in the sky somewhere over India, Penn felt loved and knew that he was truly blessed in every way. And Aria knew that her man was coming home. He fell asleep sitting up somewhere over Eastern Europe, and when they landed in France to refuel, he barely woke. Uncharacteristically, he slept almost the whole way to Washington. He almost never slept on long flights, but this was different. When they landed, he almost felt human.

Chapter Twenty

Penn and Aria had made a jump—a big jump. They knew they would not get to spend Thanksgiving or Christmas together, despite the sacrifices and the time they had spent apart. They wanted to be together, but they felt obligated to be with their respective families. Before the holiday, they would meet in NYC, Aria's best-case scenario. They would stay right off Times Square at a boutique hotel that was hip and hidden. Once again, Aria found the perfect spot. She walked around NYC and remembered how much she missed the Big Apple. That was where she grew up, and she was comfortable there. Aria and Penn went to fabulous restaurants and places that no one would have expected to find them in the city, always flying low under the radar. It made Aria so much more comfortable.

About the only high-profile thing they did during those three days was to go see the tree at Rockefeller Center. Aria actually went two more times on her own without Penn; she missed it that much. Aria's family history in NYC was actually quite substantial, and she had yet to deal with it emotionally. Aria had never told Penn about her family's history. They sat around and talked a lot, in the bedroom and in restaurants and while having tea in the afternoon. They talked while taking walks on the street and in the park. They talked on the phone when they were separated, and in his office and boardrooms all over the country. From the very beginning, they made it a priority to communicate, to try to be kind, to never yell at each other. There were times throughout the months when he would get short. Aria hated that because it hurt, and she would always call him on it. Penn would then realize what he had done and apologize. She instantly would feel better.

They lived in such a stress-filled world, but the days in New York were full of intimacy and discussions about national security and politics. The amount of targeted communication and the intellectual activity was unmatched in any other relationship either one of them had ever experienced. They could just as easily have spoken about risqué sex or science or physics and aerodynamics or medicine or national security all in the same breath. In fact, they did speak about such subjects and much more on a regular basis. Penn and Aria almost never discussed anything shallow.

Since time was their greatest friend and enemy, they never squandered it. They treated it like a piece of fragile hand-blown glass in a precious box. They guarded it with their lives. In fact, these were presents that Penn would give her when they met. First, a piece that reminded him of his mother and his grandmother, and then an ornament that had been hand-blown in Egypt.

They were goofy and insensitive together, speaking like mentally impaired people, or with accents, or like they were stoned, or like children. There was no malice intended. All in the name of play, they screwed around. They made terribly politically incorrect jokes and made fun of everyone, every single group, starting with themselves. They did things together and in front of each other that they wouldn't dream of doing in front of anyone else, a testament to the level of trust and intimacy in the relationship. People in Washington and in politics would have been mortified. Between all of the childlike, goofy behavior, they discussed, prepared, and planned things they could do in order to help steer everything that was good for the country. Their lives had become so stress-filled and so serious that they did anything they could to blow off steam. The days in New York were beautiful and amazing. Penn was finally in love with her and was able to express it. They moved about the city together and then snuggled in bed like puppies in heat.

Chapter Twenty-One

It was getting cold and grey in New York, and even though there were many more things they needed to do to learn about each other, they would have to wait. The trip ended far too soon, and they had to go home for Thanksgiving. Penn had to go back into training in order to deal with the most specialized assignment he had ever been offered. Quite frankly, nothing on earth could be compared, ever. Aria was not happy and knew what was coming and was measuring every breath, because he once again would be in a unique situation that no one would ever know about. They would be separated during the holidays, with Penn away over Christmas and New Year's. He would be in such an unbelievably hostile, uniquely dangerous environment. As usual, he would be out there all alone. He took the assignment of course, because he was the only person that the agency felt was capable of handling it and being successful.

The set up and training for the operation would be amazing. It would be at a level the agency had never seen before. They had never had this specific a problem and task to tackle before. Just the physical coordination for all the pieces to fall the way they had to in order to get him placed was absurd. Then to even get him the shot at pulling off the operation was formidable, and that did not even take into account the operation itself.

Then there was the whole issue of completing the job correctly, covering his tracks, and escaping within the proper window to avoid being tracked. The whole operation would be dangerous with a very high risk of him being killed. There were also the trips going in and out of this den of vipers, as the operatives sometimes referred to it. For those who never had to do it, this transit was always made to sound a hell of a lot easier and substantially less complicated than it actually was. For Penn, the trickiest part was covering the time away from his day job, making the excuses and building the illusion for everyone in his life to buy it.

The day came for Penn once again to head for all points unknown, and neither Penn nor Aria were looking forward to it. As usual, Aria was on the beach, waiting for Penn to leave and then to return, quite literally in one piece.

She tried to carry on her normal business and personal life while she counted the days, nights, and sometimes the moments until they got to communicate in one form or another. Until then, she pretended, just like Penn did, that things were normal. Aria never let on that she knew anything about issues of national security at the highest levels. She pretended that she was the same as the people she encountered in the office, in the mall, in the video store, or out and about. She would listen while they complained about their mostly shallow, vapid, self-centered, naïve lives—all the time thinking about all the agents in the field and the dangers they faced daily. She tried not to get irritated with people when they were so selfish and shortsighted. But there were times when she wanted to scream or ring their necks. Most of the time, she could control herself. Occasionally, she would pop off and tip her hand, after which some poor, misinformed, ignorant soul would be left standing there with their brain in their hand, quivering from too much information. Aria, like Penn, would often flash back in situations like that to when she and Penn were together, or she was alone, and she had to work hard to keep control.

One time they were in New York, hiding in a little hotel by a major university in a place where no one would ever know to look for people like them. Hiding in plain sight.

The weather was freezing, with sheets of rain coming down sideways. Penn pulled up alongside the hotel to be a gentlemen and let Aria off at the door. She begged him not to do that and told him it would turn out badly. She was adamant and almost in tears. He got a little upset and told her to get out of the car. She did what he asked, though begrudgingly.

Aria, of course, was correct, and by the time Penn got back from the car to where she was standing, there was a group of rednecks that had engaged, and Aria was ready to put her foot through a gentleman's skull in order to protect herself. Up to that point, Aria wondered what the hell was taking Penn so long and was hoping that he would speed up so she wouldn't have to do what she knew she was going to have to do. She wasn't interested in having Penn be her cleanup crew, and spending the night in the police station instead of in bed making love. Penn arrived in the nick of time, and his formidable size put an interesting twist on the whole situation. He put two and two together the second he arrived. She had run out into the rain to meet him. He saw her there vibrating in the rain, as if she were a lightning bolt in the rain, glowing on a charger. She never said a word; she never had to. He knew she wouldn't be standing there if she didn't need to be. He walked toward the building with her. He was happy that she had come out to meet him and had not taken the guy's head off. He knew better than to be around if anyone threatened his girl, because that would be like threatening him, and that would be a very bad move.

Penn understood Aria now. You do not threaten someone who has been under it, because male or female, they will do what they have to, much faster than average, and size has nothing to do with the final outcome. Penn now realized that Aria had tried to warn him. Needless to say, from then on, Penn never questioned the tiny girl again. When she balked, he always listened. He knew she never shot her mouth off. Every time she warned him about something, as far as she was concerned, her credibility was on the line. So she was never cavalier. Her only interest was to protect people. She never did it for her own benefit. After a while, Penn knew that her "abilities" and instincts, as he called them, were more accurate than any instrument. He had never seen or experienced anything quite like it. He always called when she "wanted" him to. Everyone did. She just held the phone in her hand, and it would ring nearly every time.

The intensity of this whole Christmas fiasco had left them feeling terribly guilty and frustrated. They wanted to have a place together. They wanted to be someplace different, with their own tree, and have a blended family. Both of them knew they were in the wrong place, though they never would have let their families think that they wanted to be somewhere other than where they were. They weren't even to the point of buying presents for each other for the holidays. But they were just lying to themselves, as they were way past that emotionally.

Penn made one more trip to a facility before going out on assignment, which made Aria happy. She knew where he was, and she knew he was safe. Aria loved the benefit of not having to tear her heart out for days and weeks with worry. Penn was taken care of when he was "under the wing" for a short period of time, and it calmed her. He was unique, and she trusted that his handlers would guard their investment. She also knew that they wanted to clone him. She was quite sure that the Company would have been very pleased if they decided to have some children. That would have been their best-case scenario—their babies. Cloning, no Petri dish necessary. Penn and Aria knew they would never get to do the family thing, and so they guarded their hearts. They were committed to staying busy until the time when they could finally be exactly where they wanted to be, no substitutions. They were waiting to let their lives catch up to where their hearts and minds had already started living as one. On that last trip to New York, Aria had given Penn a small token of her affection, so that he would understand her better and understand that she was already working hard to build traditions of their own. Aria gave Penn a crystal-like snowflake ornament. It sparkled and changed colors when you passed light through it. It was breathtaking. It looked like carved ice. When Aria saw it in the store, she knew she had to own it and give it to Penn. It sparkled like a diamond. Somehow it felt beautiful and precious and mushy. Aria was completely obsessed with giving it to him to put on his Christmas tree, in hopes that the following year or the year after that, it would end up on a Christmas tree they could call their own. Their first Christmas tree placed in their first house, preceded by a whole year of collecting ornaments.

These were the simple things that she dreamed of daily, for the first time in her life. The stakes got higher, physically and emotionally, for both of them every time he went out. As their lives became more intertwined and they needed each other more, they eventually reached a point where neither one could picture their life without the other in it. Their relationship became intense, and for the first time, both of these lone wolves, who never needed anyone, looked at being joined to someone at the hip as a truly viable option.

To Penn and Aria, marriage meant death. Aria had felt like this long before these days came to pass, based on her marriage and divorce, which basically equated to skydiving with no parachute a few years before. Admittedly, it still scared her beyond reproach. There was almost nothing that scared her more. She used to tell people, "Give me the gun," and then she would gesture. For Penn, he couldn't remember when he was not married; he had always been married. And he never wanted to get married again. He had been so unhappy, having made such a huge mistake and having stayed that way decades past his use-by date. Marriage was not even on his radar.

Then he met Aria, and the whole idea just flew out the window, as if the mistake had never existed. Until then, Penn and Aria had a total and complete aversion to "the M word," or "the dirty word," as Aria referred to it. It was too strong a concept for either of them. Penn got there first emotionally, in fact months before Aria, and even though they were both scared of what it might bring, they both admitted that they thought it was some place that maybe they should be. Marriage, just the thought of the word, made Aria throw up in her mouth, just a little bit. It gave her a headache and made her stomach flip-flop and sent her running for the diet soda. It upset every bodily function and gave her gas and nausea. She did not know what to do. She oscillated between almost not being able to deal with the concept to thinking it was the sexiest idea on the planet and that it should have happened already. The girl who never had problems making any kind of decision, regardless of the circumstances, was completely perplexed about the idea of marriage. Most people viewed marriage as the next logical step or as a way to have children, empowerment, money status, a regular sex partner, companionship, a visa, an identity, a change of citizenship. Few married for what Aria thought were good reasons, and Aria did not view marriage as a reason to further most of the causes. Especially the possibility of marring an agent and the pressure of becoming one yourself.

She was factoring in all the insanity and time apart, the worry, the pain, and of course the ever-present possibility of Penn coming home in a Hefty bag and her heart being broken beyond repair for all of eternity. But she was willing to entertain the idea, because she loved him and could never see loving anyone else or being loved in the same way by anyone else on the planet. She had seen too much to believe that someone else could love her like he did.

Then there was the safety—the way she felt because he was in the world in the first place. From the first moment she met him, she knew he was protecting her. Aria was used to doing all the protecting. The only person who had ever been capable of making her feel this way was her father. Now that this Freudian faux pas was sitting on her chest, she had to deal with it, and him. The part that made Aria relinquish control long enough to let someone else make her feel safe was the yummiest part of all. He was capable, and he could do it. She never had to tell him what to do; he knew. He always knew. Not only did she feel safe when she was with him, she actually was safe, and that was altogether new for Aria. He continued to prove this time and again, and it revved Aria's engines. But she never let on, or he would have done it all the time. That wasn't something he needed to foster; it was his nature. Every time he did something, she responded like Pavlov's dog and had to fight the urge to bite him and drag him to bed wherever they were. It was just so primal; she felt like she was always on the hunt for a broom closet. Miss Manners meets the broom closet. It was a constant merry war betwixt sex in safety and privacy, and primal, crazy passion, since the time they had together was always so short. It was always a combination of both.

Chapter Twenty-Two

Penn flew from New York to Canada. He had a layover, a change of venue, and then he disappeared off the face of the planet, as if he never existed. Once again he was black, blacker than black. Most people who thought they knew what was actually going on, didn't. Leaks were a constant threat, and Penn always guarded against them. So-called stories supposedly shared with a Hollywood producer who then makes a movie—more often than not, it was crap. Anyone who had access to the real deal knew it.

There are certain kinds of deeds that must be done to keep everyone alive. They never get written down in any form, ever. There are no records! But Aria knew where Penn was and what was going down and where he was headed next. He never told her, yet she managed to figure it out, as he traversed every step, across one continent after another, all the way to his destination. Further along, he made a jump to the place "where Ringo met a girl." She had her mind's eye confirmed from a comment in cyberspace. Aria and Penn knew better than to get specific in their voice and text messages, although on rare occasions, he would get careless because of extreme fatigue, and she would shoosh him. Penn never needed to go into lengthy explanations. Aria would say to Penn, "I've got it, baby." She was always afraid some bad guy would overhear him.

She picked up on all the details, even the ones referencing times when she had not been born yet. After a day, and many verbal and virtual hugs and kisses and squeezes and bytes, he arrived via a special team that he had flown with a couple of times before under similarly volatile conditions. This was the best team on the planet for this specific type of flying—flying that no one else had the experience or the balls to tackle. Despite their amazing abilities, you would think that Penn would be reticent to fly again. But he wasn't.

One of the times Penn had flown with them, one of the team's pilots had pulled a "Full Sully" and crash-landed under very harsh conditions. A lesser pilot and crew would have screwed the pooch. Obviously they lived to tell the tale, but now they had a bigger problem—survival in a subzero environment with gale-force winds. Their operation and the geography were highly classified, as in, it did not exist. There was no rescue party on speed dial; in fact, there was no speed dial. Penn was the only one who had brought along food and water. Several days elapsed before they were found, and it was Penn who provided the sustenance. His preparation and quick thinking almost always saved the day. He was known for being level. If Penn could control it, he could probably make it work, one way or another. More often than not, it was "another," because that was pretty much his daily job description. Make it work, whatever it took. This particular saga was like a bad adventure movie, so it wasn't like Penn had a hard time flying with these cats again. He had done it before, and there were no questions about anyone's abilities to make it work.

If there was any group that was set up to fly under the world's harshest conditions, it was this specific group of gentlemen. The minute Penn hit the flight line, it was like old home week for hardcore survivors. The cold and the black of this operation could not have chilled the warmth that night, because these people were family. They knew each other intimately. They had spent character-building time together over the years, on many occasions, thinking that it was "game over" multiple times, and they pulled through together. They had a great deal of respect for each other's specific abilities and personality traits, as well as love for each other as individuals. None of these guys would ever leave a man behind. They all buckled in for a long, multi-stop, challenging ride to a thankless, inhospitable environment. It would be the best part of the year to fly into the region, but to say it would be anything short of terrifying getting in or out would be delusional.

By necessity, these guys all had cast-iron stomachs, or they could not have done 99 percent of the work they performed weekly. They made the hurricane and tornado pilots look like cutesy little girls flying model airplanes. For starters, the hours these guys kept were insane, and when they worked, they almost never slept. The limits to which they regularly pushed their equipment and their bodies under extreme conditions was almost comical. A normal day at the office for them was filled with the promise of major bloodletting. Penn was strapped in and bumping around in the thin, frigid air as the aircraft fully refueled. They left the last semblance of civilization as the aircraft headed due south.

Before they took off, however, he called Aria from the flight line and thought about what wives or kids knew about what these gentlemen surrounding him did for a living. The answer was nothing. The people who loved all of these men had absolutely no clue what they really did for a living—except Aria. She knew it all. As for the rest of the group, they believed their daddy or their spouse was a pilot. They also believed a variation on a theme about Daddy being gone a few days, and then he would come back with a tan or an ice burn, which was really a compression wound or shrapnel spray, and he would share some bullshit story about being in Costa Rica or on a corporate jet job and falling while surfing. These were the stories that got shared with co-workers or by six-year-olds when they got asked by the teacher what their father's job was.

Aria told Penn months ago that the wives knew nothing about their husbands' real lives, and that all the gentlemen were immensely grateful to Penn because of his actions years before when they crashed for the first time. They were all grateful as well to the pilot who had made it possible for everyone on that plane to experience many more hugs, Christmases, sunsets, grandkids, weddings, smiles, and family times through the years. It humbled Penn and made him proud at the same time. He was happy to be a part of something bigger than himself, bigger than the time he was allotted.

After what seemed like days of no sleep and a lot of shake, rattle, and roll, they neared their destination. Tim, the pilot, landed the bird on the biggest white blanket of ice and snow you could imagine. To Penn, it felt like the surface of the moon. It was one of the scariest, most desolate and unforgiving places on the planet. Here, people really needed each other. Without the trappings of human existence, death would be swift, quiet, and ugly—unless you happened to be a polar bear's next meal.

It was so cold that any exposed skin would freeze almost immediately. They had been advised to cover up as they made their way to an all-terrain vehicle for a short trip to base camp. The party that met them on the flight line was a curious mix of multilingual scientists from around the world, as well as the project coordinator. The party that greeted them was by far the weirdest group of lab rats ever, Penn thought. He had observed from the get-go how wide-eyed and hollowed out these folks were. The base and all science projects had firm rules about how long they were allowed to remain out on any assignment. There was good reason for this; the base commander had the uncomfortable task of weeding out the "willies," as they slowly and sometimes quickly spiraled into primal, animal behaviors and madness.

People had a tendency to lose their minds there, and it did not take much to push some people over the edge. Aria warned Penn about such dangers in advance. She used the *Children of the Corn* reference, even though that was not her frame of reference. For him, a better reference was *Deliverance*. The science station's population consisted of highly intelligent, under-stimulated people in a hostile environment. Penn just happened to be the fresh meat—the journalist, as it were.

Really smart people with negative intent can do so much more damage than people of lesser intelligence. There is no contest. Penn would take stupid people on a mission all day long; they cannot do that much damage. However, someone who is bored with malice and hyper-intelligence is comparatively Hannibal Lector, and that's scary in a closed and isolated environment.

At camp, the team was greeted warmly. They were quickly fed and assigned bunks and encouraged to get some sleep. It was not a moment too soon, since everyone was almost too tired to stand. Penn needed to get rest because tomorrow it would be game on, and he had a mission to fulfill. The rest of team would get to leave tomorrow, weather-permitting. Penn was so envious he could have spit. But if he did, it would have frozen. He slept like a dead man and got up when he needed to.

After managing an uplink, he went to the main dining room and was surprised beyond belief. The suffering that was innate in the external environment was countered by the internal environment created to distract people—including fabulous food, any movie you could think of, a great library, pool tables, you name it. Everyone's personal space was cluttered with personal trinkets and knickknacks, all the things people use to express themselves. Penn was amazed at the humanity of it all in the middle of nowhere. He walked around exploring before his scheduled meeting with the site director, whom he had met last night. He learned a great deal just by saying "hello" to the people he encountered. Penn only had a rough idea of how many people were on site, so that would be a question for the upcoming meeting in about an hour.

After tooling around the vast complex and investigating a few wings, he got the lay of the land, so he wandered back to the mess hall and found his breakfast. He managed to find turkey sausage, eggs, and cereal and wash it down with some orange juice. He was famished, because flying under terrible flight conditions was not conducive to food consumption. He had not eaten well since the first flight, more than thirty-six hours ago. He helped himself to seconds and still managed to get to the director's office on time, despite getting lost twice. The place was huge and maze-like, and he was jet lagged.

In one of the hallways, he bumped into Tim, the pilot, and some of the team. They were going out later because the weather was on their side. They were on their way to the mess, and Penn was happy that they would be able to get out today. Penn wanted to go too, but like one of Snow White's seven dwarfs, Penn uttered, "Hi ho, hi ho, it's off to work we go." Everyone laughed, and Penn hustled off to his meeting. He told the guys he would see them in about ten days, if the nice weather held out. "Be safe," Tim said to Penn, looking back over his shoulder. Penn nodded, and the two had a moment as friends. "You too," Penn said. Both had big jobs ahead of them, and neither was supposed to know the true nature of the mission.

Aria was calm for the moment, knowing that Penn had arrived and had slept and eaten. She knew that he was safe, at least for a spell before things would start to get weird on the third day. Once again, she was ahead of the curve. Even though he had rested, she worried about his ability to think clearly when things started to get dicey in a few days. Penn would not be safe. He would be trapped. There would be nowhere to run or hide, nowhere to retreat to if things got really hot. Leaving the compound for any length of time meant death, plain and simple. You could not be outside, period. You could not wander from the compound. Weather and white-out conditions were daily occurrences, even at the most benign time of year. When Aria got information that was specific about a situation, she would be water-hosed, and there could be too much to process all at the same time. She would give Penn the information about what she knew in the same way. He always wrote things down when he spoke to her on the phone so that he could refer to the specific warnings she gave him. Aria was actually trying to sleep this first day, now that she knew he was in position and safe for the time being, because she knew that would not last.

Chapter Twenty-Three

The meeting with the director went well, and Penn got his interview. The director took Penn on a more exclusive tour of the facility. He filled Penn with all sorts of facts about this unique scientific station and its inhabitants and spoke about the challenges of being basically the mayor of what amounted to a small town micro-society on the tundra. Most of the facility was built well into and under the ground. He let Penn know that there was a specific rule about fraternizing between men and women, because it bred so many complications to daily life. Babies, whether you liked them or not, would be the least of the complications that would come from people having sex. In fact, to counter people's natural instincts, there was a porn room to keep the gentlemen in the facility at least semi—level. Some women used it too. There was every type of porn imaginable and a specific place to take care of business. The gentlemen were encouraged to use this room often and liberally. Penn took a pass on the option while he was a visitor, but he made sure to tell Aria all about the room because he found the concept fascinating. He felt like he was hanging out in an infertility clinic or a sperm bank.

Later that night, he saw hints of the seedy underground that was alive and well in any place on the planet where human beings were concentrated. Indeed, where there were people, there would be sex. Male and female sex, gay sex, bestiality, sex with vegetables, whatever. If you could conjure it up, there was someone, somewhere doing it. Apparently, there were scads of people there, and the vast majority were all doing it, pretty much constantly. Penn kept some strange hours, and because of his job, he learned all about the weirdness of the entire enclave, day after day. It never got dark, and the whole facility worked on a twenty-four-hour time schedule. There were shifts. It stopped down, it just never slept. The proverbial twenty-four-hour ant colony in the snow. All snow, all daylight, all the time. Penn would wake in the "middle of the night" and bust three different people sneaking back to their quarters from someone else's—doing the "walk of shame," busted by the newbie when they thought they were being so sly.

Turns out that the facility doctor was the town carnival ride and was sleeping with more people than anyone. He promised with his Hippocratic Oath to care for everyone, and apparently he really meant it! The whole facility was a Clue board game, with a serious porn element. Other than the fact that it would get wildly dangerous, Penn thought the twisted nature of the whole hostile situation was quite amusing at a visceral level. It was real and completely unreal at the same time. A total contradiction. Just like outside of the facility, it was eerily beautiful and serene, while being completely dangerous and lethal in the same breath.

Aria warned Penn about the aggressive chicks and the weirdo guys, not just the foreign operatives that would be targeting him, the scary guys that would try to ID and thwart his mission. If they managed to find him, they would surely try to bring the journalist's world to a quick and painful end. Penn knew between scoping out the place, his prep, and what he had to do that it would be pretty standard. This was his job, wherever he did his interviews, it always seemed like standard operating procedure. The director set up all of Penn's meetings with the key players in each of the departments. He cuts Penn's learning curve by saving him a great deal of time. Most of the department heads were pretty accommodating, and some could even be considered nice. Others were downright weird or spooky. By the third day, Penn had done quite a bit of checking and snooping around, looking to ID all of the necessary players in each program. His progress was swift, and someone in one of the programs came up with the idea for the journalist to be given something to really write about, showing Penn some offsite areas for study. Of course, Penn had to pretend to be amazingly positive about the prospect of an offsite field trip with a half a dozen strangers in the middle of nowhere.

Needless to say, he was not pleased, but he needed to go along and make it look good. The drill when this happened was that the director gave someone in the group a high-powered rifle, because there was the problem of free-range polar bears that liked to feast on humans who got careless outside. At daybreak, Penn woke and contacted the home office to let Clay know what time this fabulous trip was supposed to commence so they could keep an eye on the party. A tall, lanky guy got issued the rifle. This made Penn wary, but he kept his anxieties concealed. Everyone readied themselves for the trip that would take about three or four hours. Once underway, they traveled about an hour away from the enclave—a long way from home base. Penn pretended to be jacked out of his mind about the amazing landscape and the beauty and majesty of it all. But all he wanted was to keep an eye on the guy with the gun, get back to base, drink some hot cocoa, and take a hot shower. The days were ticking away, and Penn just wanted to finish up his interviews, hit his target, write his story, and fly the fuck home. The team got back from the day trip, and no visitors or polar bears had been harmed.

The minute they got within sight of the facility, visibility started to deteriorate. Throughout their excursion, they were equipped with radios, and the weather station kept the team leader abreast of the coming fronts. With no geographical barriers and such a large land mass, fronts would come fast and furious, and you could be in an awful situation within minutes. As a result, ventures outside the compound to monitor or repair various instruments, as well as flights in and out, had to be flexible and well-coordinated. You had to remain in constant contact with the base and not go too far, or you could get lost and perish. It would be akin to being adrift in space, cut loose from the space station, adrift, until you died. The blue and white sky with the yellow-white base was amazing to stare at from far away. As they got closer to home, they could almost feel the heat and energy humming under the ice and snow. They could feel the fact that there was life out here buried somewhere under the snow. It was definitely the energy that attracted the animals, because out here, there was absolutely nothing, and it gave a whole new meaning to the word desolate.

Penn had never spent so much time on a snow vehicle with big belted tires as he just had. Never in his life before did he have occasion to test the true performance of such specific land gear. But he did have more than a passing familiarity with high-powered rifles used for stopping humans and free-range predators. Despite his many exploits in unforgiving environments the world over, these

situations were unique watermarks for him.
Experience. There was no substitute for it.

Aria was pacing the floor at home, waiting to hear that
no one had been shooting at Penn and that he had
arrived safely back at base, and he could chug hot
cocoa and get warm again. She was waiting for the big
satellite in the sky to tell her everything was going to
be okay. Penn, relieved by the successful outing, made
his way to his bunk and checked in with Clay. He
changed into his workout clothes to hit the gym, after
first inhaling some protein bars and a protein shake.

At the gym, he encountered some of the most overt,
bizarre behavior of the entire trip. The guys tended to
be very brusque and territorial—even physical about
inflicting pain. Penn made it very clear without using
language that he would not be tolerating that today
or for the remainder of his trip. When he was working
out, he also attracted a few of the more aggressive
females Aria had warned him about. One girl even
followed him into the locker room. He told her to back
off. He wanted to be left alone and get back to his
quarters to plan his next few days and get some sleep.

Since things had started to get more unsettled,
there was a buzz that now existed about his visit.
People were starting to take notice, and many of
them apparently were not happy. It amused him how

strident and what bad actors people were. People were either very happy to meet someone from outside, or they were upset, territorial, and had issues. Penn had a specific task—to find some folks who had been charged with some very dirty work. These people were passing information to foreign governments and messing with national security at a high level. Whoever these people were, they fit Penn's definitions of scumbag. All these low-level head cases in this frigid ant farm just ticked him off and made him intolerant. And now that people had started to become overt in their aggressiveness and tried to lord themselves over him, it just pissed him off that much more.

Penn took his personal freedom, his personal space, internal and external, and the use and control of his physical body very seriously; he had worked too hard to attain all of it. When anyone tried to impede his personal progress by exacting control over him, it became unacceptable very quickly. Penn was not the kind of guy you wanted to be on the bad end of; you would lose, regardless of who you were or what advantage you thought you had. You would lose. That's why he was there in the first place, because he did not lose.

It was this faith that kept Aria so deeply tied to Penn when he was in the field, because she was not in the habit of losing either. She did whatever was necessary in order to make it work. Discomfort was never an issue. Both viewed their lives through the prism of taking awful medicine as a child. You just did it. The issue was the outcome, not the discomfort on the way to the outcome. Penn was weeding out the people he did not need to be in front of in each department. He packed small, quiet weapons, no guns, because even if they are silenced, they still make noise, and there is a scent. Penn needed stealth weapons.

His hands and body were quite effective, as were a few other tools of the trade. Penn was quite sure things would get ugly, and sooner than he originally thought. That was the constant struggle in the field; you had to be able to assess in real time the unfolding of an assignment while you were eyeball deep in it. This was easier to say than to actually execute successfully. Timing was everything.

Being too close, getting too involved, or being emotionally attached was always a danger. It clouded your decision-making process and was almost never a good thing. Penn turned on the television to obscure the sound of his voice because it was time to call Langley and discuss a new plan of attack. The peace of mind he had earlier in the operation was a big benefit now. It made sleep and safety possible, and neither could be assured the next two or three days. Clay and Penn had a decent conversation for the first time in days, thanks to clearer than usual weather. Penn was convinced that during the interviews over the past few days, he had been "made," and it was now imperative that things move forward. The team was standing by and in place. Penn was preparing for closing in on a person he thought was the target. Not until everything was actually in play would the target become aware. By then, it would be too late for the target to do anything about his imminent expiration. Clay was happy about the progress and was watching the weather because there was a violent storm moving in. Penn and Clay and the team at Langley had been monitoring NOAA, and Clay could not guarantee how everything would stack up—including when he would be able to get a team in to extract Penn when things got very dangerous. Penn would be on his own, without a means of escape for at least forty-eight hours, maybe longer.

Aria got the mental brief about the weather. She woke and ran to her computer, checking for updates and to see whether or not she was correct. She went to NOAA and then to a handful of satellite photos. All hunches confirmed, Aria saw that he would be stuck. She drew a deep breath. *Here we go again,* she thought to herself. He wouldn't be getting out anytime soon. He would be doing his job and earning his keep times ten times over. Penn and Clay changed the M.O. of the operation and made a pact: the cleanup team and the transportation specialists were going to be unavailable for comment.

Penn was given the blanket mission statement of "whatever it takes." It was game on. His forum, duty, parameters, and means for accomplishing a goal all shifted. When Clay and Penn wrapped up the conversation, Penn knew what had to be done. He packed his pockets, grabbed his briefcase, and went to the lab, where he was greeted by one of the chicks who had hit on him earlier in week. She walked by him on the way out the door and subtly gave him the finger. He just smiled. He went to see the section director and asked to see two different guys who worked under him and for an empty conference room. Penn left the lab and went to the empty conference room. The director sent the first guy in to see Penn. The guy came in and sat down, getting more uncomfortable as Penn asked him a series of probing questions. He was an unimposing, Eastern European man who looked like a weasel to Penn.

When the interview was over, the little man scurried out of the room like a rat. Penn heard him through the bug he had planted on him when he walked into the room. The human weasel called his contact the minute he left the room. Penn now had conformation that the second guy he called for had absolutely no intention of showing up for his "interview." Penn left the room and decided to let the bastards stew. He wanted to see what they would do next. He headed for the cafeteria to get some lunch, after which he would do a quick workout to kill the stress. He walked by the window and shook his head, as he could see everything he and Clay discussed. It was crazy white-out conditions as far as the eye could see. Penn ate alone in a corner and then stuffed some granola and snacks into his pockets to take back to his room. Just because he had hidden weapons and a license to kill didn't mean he had to go hungry.

Penn was smart enough to know that after he spoke to the second guy, eating and drinking would become markedly less safe as the hours and days wore on. In these type of situations, you had better know who could be aligned with whom and who could have access to which departments. Penn knew just how much these people hated him and what a poisoning spree they had been on for a few years around the world. So far he had managed to avoid everything despite being in some very compromising positions. He went back to his quarters and blew off the idea of the workout. He needed to make things appear normal to everyone at the compound, so he quickly put in another call to Clay and told him what he intended to do. He dropped off his briefcase and was unpacking when Clay told him the weather would be terrible for the next twelve to sixteen hours. He also told him that

the aircraft, one of two planes that had the ability
to get in, was having mechanical trouble. They were
getting their hands on the parts and fixing it, but it
would be at least twenty-four hours. He told Penn to
watch his ass and to make sure he got it done. Clay
told Penn that he would be monitoring the weather
and the entire situation, and that he would get him
out of there as fast as humanly possible. He also told
Penn he would meet him at the first refueling stop.
They agreed on a time to speak again within a few
hours.

Penn set up his quarters with a series of devices to
make sure his quarters could not be breached without
his knowledge. Then he went out into the hallway
and started to hunt for his other target, the big fish.
After checking a few places, Penn found him in one of
the bathrooms. He confronted him. After locking the
bathroom door, Penn asked him about his position
in the whole setup, but the guy would reveal nothing,
including his accomplice. It didn't really matter; Penn
had already put it together anyway. Still, he did not
pull any punches, literally or figuratively. The guy
felt so threatened that he tried to get physical. Penn
quietly put a stop to that; with two sharp blows to the
head, he knocked him out. Penn put him in a stall and
planted a bug on him. Since there was nowhere to run,
Penn would take care of business tomorrow.

Penn would need to find a way out as soon as possible after he sanctioned his target, so it didn't make a whole lot of sense to overreact now. Once he completed his mission, there would be no way to deny it and nowhere to go. And who knows, the guy might still fess up, and that would change things. For now, there was no way to tell. These circumstances allowed Penn some breathing room. Penn arranged himself and unlocked the door, left the bathroom, and walked to the chow hall. He picked up more food, making sure the cameras caught him, and said hello to some of the nicer people he had met. This established even more time stamps. Penn had been cataloging all the cameras and their movements for eleven days.

He returned to the room and shot a text off to tell Clay what was up and check on the latest on the flight schedule. Penn spent the evening in his quarters monitoring the bugs he had planted. He also monitored the updates on the weather. Later, he decided that the target was screwing up and was not going to be coming to Jesus on his own. He was going to have to stop the bleeding and send him to Jesus tonight, before he could get any more Intel to the bad guys. He would also have to let his other people at the facility know what was going on. Then there would be no question about Penn's cover being blown or people left alive to talk about it.

Penn crawled into bed for a few hours for some much deserved sleep. First, he set up the room in case anyone tried to gain entry while he was asleep and vulnerable. Then he shot Aria a text and drifted off. Aria was up pacing, ahead of the storm, concentrating on helping Penn and finally getting past the hubbub of Christmas. She knew what was coming and spent time putting out the energy while Clay and his team did the prep work for Penn being under it again in a few hours. Clay was hurriedly getting the airplanes online and coordinated for the swoop, scoop, and the rendezvous at the first refueling stop. Aria wanted everything to go perfectly; it had to. There was a very small safety window, due to weather and because of the nature of the operation. Aria had no input from Penn and was trying desperately to set up his homecoming. In her mind's eye, she could see how he was getting out. She was just a little fuzzy on exactly when, but that would become clearer over the next few hours as she concentrated more on Penn and on Clay's behavior.

Chapter Twenty-Four

A few hours passed, and Penn shook himself awake. Aria took a deep breath and almost fell over. She knew he was awake and they were online. It was game on. Within minutes, everything would culminate.

Aria dropped what she had been working on and went to her bedroom to be alone. She needed to focus. Penn sat up in bed and all but jumped up to pee and shower. He brushed his teeth, showered, toweled off, and ate a protein bar. He knocked back some orange juice while he planned the backup to his backup weapon. He packed a small black bag and put his all-weather gear into the bag to hide it. After stuffing food into his pockets, he shot Clay a text. Then he sent Aria a text and told her, "I love you." It had a half-hour delay getting to her, but she already knew. Penn left the room in his many black layers and found the candidate in a far-flung lab on the outskirts of the compound, hiding. It was the middle of the facility's night, and the crews on duty were lean. Penn planned it that way. He entered the lab, and of course John was the only guy there, hiding out amongst the test tubes. A scuffle ensued, but Penn was careful not to make any noise or break glass. Sound travels in the dead of night, especially in concrete and metal boxes underground in the middle of nowhere. He could not afford a screw-up, not today.

Penn put the bad guy down silently. He would no longer be selling secrets that didn't belong to him. Penn felt good about it. This facility existed to keep the world safe, not to assist in making it less safe. By now, the rescue fly boys were about an hour and a half out, and the weather was breaking and bumpy. They were flying in between fronts, just as Clay had planned. Aria was pacing and breathing hard. She knew what was going down. Penn threw his unconscious adversary over his shoulder and took him to a snowmobile that he had hidden around the back of the compound. He strapped him on and double-checked the full gas tank. Then he cranked it up and pointed the nose toward the base of the mountains in the distance. He took a breath, and it all but froze coming out of his mouth. Carefully, he timed his departure to avoid the closed circuit cameras. As he sped away from the compound into the middle of nowhere, he was never so aware of his mortality. But he felt a surge of warmth and electrical energy rush through his core, and he knew by now that the source was Aria. She always helped; she was right there. She never let him down or made him do anything alone, and he no longer wanted to.

Penn had to make this snowmobile run, and he had to be successful. The plans had changed, and it was up to him to clean up the mess for the world. It was insanely scary out there, and Penn felt small and insignificant.

He went twenty-five minutes to the base of the mountain range before the snow was too deep to ride further on. At that point, he turned the snowmobile north and went a few miles more. Then he made sure John met someone's maker. Penn was pretty sure that after Jesus found out what John tried to pull off, he wouldn't be the one waiting for John. Penn looked around at the majesty of the frigid natural surroundings. Then he straddled the snowmobile and blasted off once again, lit only by the moon and the glow on the horizon, retracing his route.

The wind started to pick up. Within a few hours, the sun would rise higher in the sky. It started to snow ever so gently, and Penn took a breath. Back at home, Aria was sitting on her bed, slowly coming down, breathing slowly, fully aware and wide eyed. Clay was getting into an unmarked government airplane. The fly boys had just contacted the tower, or what was used as the tower at base camp, and notified them that they would be on the ground in about twenty-five minutes. They would be refueling the minute they hit the packed ice. The recovery team would land, gather supplies and mail, use the toilet, eat, and collect their precious cargo, Penn. The snow was coming down lightly when they pulled in, and visibility was good for now.

Penn had been back for about ten minutes. After he stashed the snowmobile, he made a beeline for his quarters. He showered to get warm. Then he quickly packed and went to the mess to make sure that he had been seen by the scientists and the video surveillance. He swallowed some turkey sausage and some eggs. He missed Aria, and he was cold, so he was drinking tea and cocoa. As he was dunking his toast, Captain Tim and the team walked into the mess hall. He was never so happy to see people he cared about. He jumped up to hug Tim and asked when they were leaving. He let them know that he was ready when they were. He did not want there to be any miscommunication. Captain Tim did not know what the operation involved; it was need-to-know only. He just knew he was supposed to deliver Penn to the rendezvous point where Clay would be waiting. Penn excused himself and went to bid the facility director farewell. He also had to call Clay and let him know they were leaving.

Within an hour, they were all on the flight line, and he was all but jumping up and down with glee. The pilots did their last-minute flight checks, and Penn strapped himself in and said a silent prayer. He hated flying, especially under these conditions, but still he was grateful for his full belly, and he was curious to see how long that happiness about his breakfast lasted. Under these flying conditions, it could go either way. The crew and the passengers were cleared by the tower for takeoff, and the captain guided the aircraft down the icy runway. Captain Tim forced the plane into the sky, and as it climbed, he retracted the gear. About an hour into the flight, everyone on the plane got airsick. The turbulence was terrible. Even Tim started having thoughts about crash landing. Everyone threw up, one by one. Dry heaves became the rule. The flight was frightening and violent. When they finally landed to refuel, they all would have liked to have spent the night. But they had a schedule they had to keep. It was all very carefully timed. Penn wanted to text Aria, but Clay advised him against it. Aria would have to wait until the next refueling stop, where he would meet Clay.

Penn said his good-byes to Captain Tim and the recovery team, and they had a good laugh about everyone losing their lunch and their breakfast, but unlike last time, Captain Tim was able to keep the airplane in the air. And Clay didn't have to rescue his rescuers again. As if on cue, Clay and his team met Penn to lead him out to yet another flight line where a private jet was ready for them. They boarded for a short hop to a safe place where they would spend the night and debrief before returning to Washington the next day. They also spent one night on the way home doing research for the next field trip. Clay and Penn were mindful of the fact that they were on the federal payroll. Contrary to popular belief, these case officers were respectful of who was paying the bills. In fact, they were much more aware of it than most federal workers, because they understood what it was like to be stuck in a foreign land with no resources.

Aria slept like a baby that night and then prepped to board a flight the next day for Reagan National Airport in Washington. When she arrived at baggage claim, she was met by an unmarked black sedan. A nameless man greeted her and confirmed why she was there. Together, they made the forty-five-minute drive to Andrews Air Force Base. She knew Penn was glued to his window during the flight as they flew in over the DC area. They had missed the holiday season together, so Penn was melancholy. He missed her terribly. Clay knew what he had to do; he had arranged to have Aria deposited with a handler onto an airstrip. A massive, grey, four-engine cargo aircraft pulled up. The ground crew scurried in the light snow. Illuminated by the lights from the Escalade, steps dropped from the door of the airplane. Out came Penn, followed by Clay. Aria could barely believe her eyes. Penn's face lit up as he descended onto the tarmac. Aria slowly approached him and buried her face in his chest. He wrapped his entire body around her as snowflakes fell all around them.